David O'Malley is a former Minor League baseball pitcher turned Anglican Priest who is fed up with the pettiness and hypocrisy of organized religion. He's conflicted about his priestly vocation.

Hannah and David fall in love when they join forces to save two neglected lions from a roadside zoo. But when Hannah's profession becomes known, the Church orders David to end his relationship with her.

Will David choose passion or the priesthood? Can love be a gateway to freedom for two people who are both imprisoned by their own loneliness?

Caged Lions Never Roar
Copyright © 2019 Arthur Archambeau
ISBN: 978-1-4874-2312-4
Cover art by Martine Jardin

Published by eXtasy Books Inc or
Devine Destinies, an imprint of eXtasy Books Inc

Look for us online at:
www.eXtasybooks.com or www.devinedestinies.com

Caged Lions Never Roar

By

Arthur Archambeau

DEDICATION

For Eugene B. Larkin Jr., AKA **Big Slim***, who left this world way too soon on 12 December 2018. He loved all animals and was everything that a man is supposed to be.*

CHAPTER ONE: BOBBY AND BABS

Their names were Bobby and Babs and they spent their days pacing back and forth in a habitat no bigger than a two-car garage. Two four-year-old African lions who had spent their entire lives in captivity. They were the star attractions of Colonel Rupert's Wildlife Wonderland Zoo, a small, roadside zoo in Baltimore. There was a wading pool in their enclosure filled with filthy water. Bobby and Babs never used it. Lions, unlike tigers, don't like water. Colonel Rupert, evidently, wasn't aware of that.

Hannah Cohen stood in front of the enclosure, sipping her coffee and shaking her head. "Oh, Bobby! It looks like you're getting mange. And Babs, you're limping today. Do they ever have a vet come in here to look at you two?" she wondered aloud. She shivered in the chill of early April in Maryland and wished she had worn her mittens and a stocking cap.

Hannah was twenty-six years old, shoulder-length blonde hair, sky blue eyes, with an athletic build. A dead ringer for a young Debbie Gibson, she wore a red University of Maryland hoodie, faded blue jeans, white sneakers, and a pink Orioles cap. Her ponytail stuck out from the open back end of the cap. Dangling from her wrist was a rope. Attached to the rope was a white bar of soap.

As she watched the lions pace, a tear raced down her cheek. She made a weekly visit to the zoo to check on Bobby and Babs and every week she cried when she saw them. This day she cried especially hard because she could see that the

1

lions were deteriorating, both physically and mentally. She sniffled and searched her purse for a tissue.

"Here you go. I've got you covered." A large hand offering a travel size pack of tissue appeared in her peripheral vision. Hannah turned her head and saw him. He was very tall, about six-feet-four-inches, she guessed, late twenties, athletic build, auburn hair, royal blue eyes, deep tan. She took a deep breath and caught a whiff of his cologne. It smelled like chocolate, almost like a bakery. He was wearing a white dress shirt underneath a powder blue, cashmere V-neck sweater, black gabardine trousers, and a pair of shiny black penny loafers. On his left ring finger, he wore a huge gold ring with a black onyx stone. The ring is gauche, she thought. A little too Wise Guy-ish, but it wasn't a wedding ring. She thought he looked like a 1960s hipster crooner — the kind who had an effortless, velvety voice. The kind who could sing you to sleep with some tender, romantic lullaby. Yes, he looked like a singer from a bygone era, dressed for his album cover photo shoot. All he needed was a lit cigarette between his fingers.

"Here, you can have the whole pack. I got an entire case of them at the wholesale club the other day," he told her.

Really? Who buys an entire case of tiny packs of tissues?

She took the pack of tissues, opened it, and dabbed her eyes as she sniffled. "Thank you. I don't mean to make a spectacle of myself, but I come here every week and I get so emotional when I see these beautiful animals living like this."

"This is my first time here, but I'm appalled by what I see," he said.

"So you have a problem with this, too?" she asked. She was excited at the prospect of finding someone who was as offended by the conditions as she was.

"Yes. I love animals and I hate to see them suffer. And these poor lions are suffering. I saw some pictures of this place online and had to come and see if it was really as bad as it looked." He glanced at the pacing lions, then added, "And it is."

"I come here every week to check on Bobby and Babs. Part of me hates doing it because every time I come and pay the admission fee, I'm putting money in old man Rupert's pocket, but I have to see my Bobby and Babs. I just have to," she said.

He shook his index finger for emphasis, "You know, one thing I've already noticed is that I haven't heard either of them roar."

"Oh, and you won't. They don't roar. Neither of them. I've been visiting them every week for over a year now and have never once heard a roar. Another thing, they're male and female yet they've never mated, never produced a single cub."

"That's sad."

"Yes. It is," she agreed.

He extended his hand. "Oh, by the way, I'm David. David O'Malley."

She shook his large, warm hand. "I'm Hannah Cohen. Nice to meet you." *He's cute, very cute. Even if he does look like he could have been the sixth member of The Rat Pack.*

"That's, uh, an interesting bracelet you have there." He pointed to the soap-on-a-rope hanging around her wrist.

"Ah, yeah. Good luck charm. Yep. My good luck charm." She nodded emphatically. *There is no way I'm getting into that whole issue now.*

"Well, it's more original than a four-leaf clover, that's for sure." He moved on. "You know, someone should do something about this place. The conditions are horrible, but it doesn't look like anyone's doing anything to force a change."

"It's legal, perfectly legal. Colonel Rupert's meeting the minimum standards according to the law. Animals don't have many rights, so the standards are low. In the eyes of the regulators, housing lions like this is acceptable."

"That may be true, but there are still things that could be done. You know, get the press to come out here and document the conditions. Write letters to the editor. Start a petition. If they get enough bad publicity and public pressure, they might clean up their act. Or even agree to let the lions go to a real wildlife refuge, where they'd have plenty of room."

She shrugged her shoulders. "Yeah, but it's such an uphill battle. I've thought of all those things before, but what can one person do?"

"A lot. Time and time again, the world's been changed by a solitary person with a passion to right a wrong. Why, look at Jackie Robinson."

She nodded. "That's true. But nowadays people don't care."

"You have to make them care. You have to make your passion contagious." There was a brief pause and he looked her in the eye. "What do you say, Hannah Cohen, beneficiary of my wholesale club membership, why don't you and I change the world? Or at least our little corner of it. You know, make it our project—our mission—to get Bobby and Babs into a better situation. So they can roar. Sound cool?"

She was impressed. *He's not only cute but seems like a stand-up guy. Pretty rare. Of course, he might be playing my emotions to try to get into my pants. He is, after all, a man.*

"Well . . . sure, sure. I guess. But where would we even start?"

"We should have a strategy session, to brainstorm ideas. What are you doing next Sunday? Sunday afternoon, that is."

"I'm actually off Sundays."

"Great. I'm starting a two-week vacation next Sunday afternoon so what do you say we get together for lunch? My treat."

"Um, yeah, I guess . . . I guess I could do that. I guess."

"Are you familiar with the city? You know Tiffany's Diner? On Loch Raven Boulevard."

"Yeah. I know Tiffany's. I eat there a lot."

"I do, too. Best diner food in Baltimore. How about if we meet at Tiffany's at noon? I'll bring some yellow legal pads and pens for both of us, so we can write our ideas down. I swear you come up with better ideas when you write on those official yellow legal pads." He smiled at her.

He has a nice smile, a kind smile. White teeth, too. But not that hideous, fluorescent, glowing white that you see with people who have their teeth whitened. But that tan! That's a tanning salon tan if ever I saw one. He looks like Snooki.

She nodded. "Yeah. Sounds good."

They exchanged phone numbers and email addresses.

"Well, listen, it was great meeting you, Hannah. I've got to get back to the office. I'll look forward to seeing you on Sunday." There was a pause. "I mean, I'll look forward to generating ideas. I didn't mean that I was looking forward to seeing *you*, per se." There was another pause. "Not that there's anything wrong with seeing you. I mean, you're nice to see. Nice to look at, that is. Not that I was looking at you or anything. Of course, you *would* be worth looking at." He was blushing. Finally, he said, "Okay, um, I'm going to shut up now and leave."

She laughed. *Aw, he's tripping over his tongue. Cute. This guy's much too clumsy to be a player.* "It's okay, David. Really, it is. I know what you mean. I'll definitely look forward to having lunch with you on Sunday."

"You will?"

"I will." She nodded and smiled.

"Okay. Well, Hannah Cohen, I'll see you on Sunday." He backed up and gave her the double finger, six-shooter point.

Oh, Lord! We're going to have to do something about this image of yours. Way too Goodfellas, honey. I'm not sure if you're saying goodbye to me or giving a signal to some guy named Carmine to come out of the bushes and whack me. As he backed up, he slipped in a pile of horse manure. She laughed.

"Dammit! These were brand new penny loafers, too," he muttered.

"We'll put that in our report that Colonel Rupert is leaving animal feces in public places. Thus, creating a safety and health hazard," she said.

As he rubbed his foot along the ground to try to get the poop off his shoes, he told her, "Right. That's why I did that. I intentionally stepped in that mess to demonstrate the filthy nature of this place."

"Oh, I'm sure it was a calculated move on your part." She guffawed.

He smiled an easy smile. "I'll see you. It was a pleasure to meet you." She nodded.

She watched as he walked away. *Is this the one who will understand?*

Chapter Two: "This Church Does Not Buy Medicine for Cats"

David passed Mrs. Willoughby, the Church administrator, going up the stairs to his office on the second floor of the parish house. "Bishop Higgins is waiting in your office. He doesn't look happy."

"Is he ever happy?" David asked.

"Just trying to give you the heads-up, Father O'Malley," she said.

"Yeah. I know. Thanks."

When he got to his office door, he took a deep breath and crossed himself. *It's showtime. Drama one-oh-one from freshman year in college, don't fail me now.*

He opened the door. "Bishop Higgins, so good to see you, sir." He extended his hand.

The bishop, a balding, bearded man in his late 40's, looked at his expensive watch. "You're late. I've been sitting here for a good fifteen minutes." David kept his hand extended for a few seconds, then awkwardly withdrew it.

"My apologies, sir. But I stopped to talk to this guy. A homeless vet, the guy fought in Iraq. He was hungry, so I took him to a fast food joint and got him something to eat."

"Um-hum. Probably on dope. A lot of those homeless, vagabond types are, you know." *Dope? This guy sounds like a nineteen fifties PSA, the kind where the announcer would say, "Now, don't forget kids — dope is for dopes."*

"Well, sir, the issue of drug addiction is a whole different can of worms."

"They need to get tough on these alleged *addicts*. Send a few of them up the river for life without parole and I guarantee you, this so-called drug epidemic would stop. They coddle them too much. Of course, that's what I think. If you ask me."

"But I didn't ask you. Sir."

The bishop smiled a tense smile. "So you didn't." There was an awkward pause before the bishop continued, "Tell me, how long have you been ordained?"

"For about two years now. You know that."

The bishop pointed at him. "Right. In other words, long enough to know how things work. Long enough to know what is and what is not permissible."

"What are you driving at, sir?"

The bishop pulled out a small, spiral notepad from the pocket of his purple clerical shirt. "I, ah, I have some things to discuss with you. Some irregularities."

David sat down at his desk chair, let out a sigh, and crossed his arms. "Okay. Let's hear them."

"I was reviewing St. Anne's financial expenditures from last month. I can see that one-hundred dollars went to a Charm City Veterinary Clinic. The note here says something about Mikey's medication. Explain please."

"Well, sir, Mikey's a cat—belongs to Mrs. Levine. She's a widow. On a fixed income. Mikey has a heart condition and needs a medication called Pimobendan. He would die without it. Mrs. Levine loves that cat. He's all she has, and the medication is pretty expensive. So I approved an outreach offering for her to cover it."

"Ah-ha. Well, I looked into this Mrs. Levine. Her name does not appear in the Church membership directory."

"No, she's not a member. She's Jewish."

"Well, I figured that much, with a name like Levine." The bishop threw up his hands with his palms facing away from his body, as if preparing to defend himself. "Not that there's anything wrong with that, mind you. I eat at Jewish delis all the time. Those people make excellent sandwiches. Still, she's not supporting this Parish with any donations. Moreover, this Church does not buy medicine for cats."

"But, sir, the Outreach Fund has over a million dollars in it. We're not hurting for money here. What good is having all that money if you can't use it to do some good?"

The bishop's temper flared. "I didn't say that it shouldn't be used! I said it shouldn't be used for a damn cat who's owned by a J—"

Almost said it, didn't you?

The bishop took a deep breath, like someone who had barely avoided a catastrophe. Finally, he finished his thought, "By someone who isn't a member of the Church."

"What else is on that list of yours?"

"I understand you brought that mangy, flea-infested Pitbull of yours to the Sunday morning service a few weeks ago. True?"

"She doesn't have mange or fleas. Before I adopted her from the shelter, someone poured chemicals on her and burned her. That's why she's missing all that fur on her back. I made her part of my sermon, to show the congregation that they shouldn't judge anyone based on reputation. I wanted everyone to see that Pitbulls can be good, gentle dogs, that they shouldn't be condemned because of their breed. Just like people shouldn't be judged based on superficial criteria. That's a very biblical message, as far as I'm concerned."

"And if she had bitten anyone during your little show-and-tell session, the Church would have been liable."

"But she wouldn't bite anyone. She's never even growled at anyone."

"I'm not going to sit here and argue it with you, Father

O'Malley. I'm ordering you to never let it happen again."

"What else?"

"Keeping the Church unlocked and opened twenty-four hours a day. That must stop."

David threw his hands up in the air. "What's wrong with that? We need to be accessible to people."

"There are valuables in there. That silver communion chalice goes back to the early eighteenth century. It's priceless. Opening the door to the riffraff twenty-four/seven means it's only a matter of time before those valuables disappear."

"Bishop Higgins, do you want me to serve God and His people or be the curator of a museum?"

"You're being insolent. I am, after all, your boss."

David emphatically shook his head. "Wrong. You're not my boss."

"No? If I'm not, then who is?"

"A Jewish carpenter who opened doors to people rather than locking them out, liked animals, hung out with the *riffraff*, and as far as I know, never gave any money to this Church. Now, are there any other issues? Sir."

The bishop got up and stuck his finger in David's face. "You had better watch yourself. Because I'll be watching you. You know, for someone so young, you're very cocky. And cockiness is a vice. A sin, in fact."

"Are we done?"

"For now. I expect you to follow my directives. I'll show myself out." As he walked out, he stepped in some of the residual horse manure that had come off David's shoes when he entered the office. The bishop raised his shoe and touched it, evidently thinking it was only mud.

The bishop raised his hand to his nose. "This is shit! I've got shit on my shoe and now it's on my finger. I've got to get all washed up."

"According to the rumors, you already are," David quipped.

"Like being the smartass, don't you? These shoes I have on—they cost five-hundred dollars. And now they've got shit on them. They're ruined!"

"Five-hundred, you say? I thought only televangelists could afford shoes that expensive. Do you drive a Mercedes, too?"

"Good-day, Father O'Malley."

Jerk.

David looked out the window, into the parking lot, as Bishop Higgins got into his car. "I'll be damned," he muttered. "He *is* driving a Mercedes."

After Higgins' car pulled out, David went out to the parish house back porch. He took out his pack of Camel cigarettes and tapped one out. He lit it up and deeply inhaled. *If only I hadn't torn my rotator cuff. Maybe I'd be pitching at Camden Yards for the Orioles. Instead, I'm stuck here playing politics within an institution that's supposed to be doing God's work but is like any other big corporation. Just as petty. Just as superficial. Just as screwed-up. I can't wait for my vacation to start.*

Then he thought about his upcoming lunch date with Hannah. And he smiled.

CHAPTER THREE: POLECATS

Friday night. A busy work night for Hannah. She made good money working the 6 PM to 2 AM shift. She sat at the makeup mirror backstage and applied the tools of her trade. At an adjacent mirror, Nicki, a twenty-nine-year-old brunette, whose selling points were her huge boobs, husky voice, and twerking skills, did the same.

"I hate my boobs, Hannah. They're too damn big. Now, yours are perfect. They're big, but not, like, ginormous. You've got nice areolas and nipples, too."

"Thanks." Hannah looked down at them.

"I had a cheeseburger yesterday and I feel guilty as hell. I'm, like, three pounds over my ideal weight," Nicki told her as she curled her hair.

"You look great," Hannah assured her.

"Easy for you to say. Your body is perfect. Perfect tits, perfect ass, perfect legs, perfect teeth, perfect hair, perfect weight. Every guy in Baltimore wants to hit that. Hell, if I were a guy, I'd want to hit that."

"I'm not perfect. My legs are too short, my lips aren't nearly as full and pouty as yours, and my neck is too long."

"You're just being polite," Nicki told her.

Hannah wanted the subject to change and decided to unleash the juicy tidbit of information she'd been hoarding. "So . . . I met a guy this week."

"Did you, now?"

"Yup. We're meeting for lunch on Sunday to try to figure out a way to help those two lions in that horrid zoo that I was telling you about. But I'd be willing to mix business and pleasure." She grinned a mischievous grin.

"Good for you, honey. What's he like?"

"Cute. And nice. At least he seems nice so far."

"Give him time. I'm sure his inner jerk will surface soon enough."

"You say that like you hope that happens, like you want the rest of us to be as miserable as you are."

Nicki put down her curling iron and looked at Hannah. "No. That's not true. It's just that girls like us are in an awful situation. We're damaged goods. Let's assume for a minute, this guy . . . does he have a name?"

"David."

"Okay, let's assume this David character is decent. Different from the rest of his species. He's not going to beat you. Not going to cheat on you. Not going to try to control you. Let's assume that this guy is Mister Wonderful. That he'd bring you flowers for no special reason. And hold you by a roaring fire on a cold winter day. And take care of you when you had the flu even if that meant catching it himself. Sounds good, huh?"

As Nicki spoke, Hannah was conjuring up corresponding images in her mind.

"Uh huh." She placed both hands over her heart and sighed.

"And what happens when he finds out you're a stripper—the headline attraction, no less—at Polecats Gentleman's Club, a place that, by the way, is completely and totally devoid of anyone who could even remotely be considered a gentleman."

"It's not like I'm proud of this. You know that I hate it."

"You say that, but you're not under contract so you could quit anytime you wanted. So . . . why don't you?"

"Because I have bills to pay and I don't know how to do

anything else. That degree in English isn't worth much in the real world."

"You're making too much out of this, taking it too seriously. We're not doing anything illegal and it's a free country after all."

Hannah got angry. "Yeah. A free country. We have the freedom to shake our tits and asses in the faces of drunk truck drivers for money. Makes me sick! Almost literally. We're not free. This life that we're living . . . it's a prison, not freedom. At least that's what it is to me."

"You still haven't answered my question—what are you going to do when Mister Wonderful finds out you're a stripper? And don't say he won't because he will. You'll be out in a restaurant, having a romantic dinner, and some slimeball who recognizes you will come up and grab your tit or something. And it'll be like the last guy you dated six months ago. You know, the lawyer who wanted to run for Congress. What happened with him? Hmm?" She didn't even give Hannah a chance to respond. "He dumped you once he found out because you were only going to drag him down, even after you told him you'd quit. Like I said—you and me—we're damaged goods."

"You had to bring up the lawyer, didn't you? Maybe this one will be different. Maybe he won't care what other people think. He doesn't seem to care much about that type of thing from what I've seen so far. Maybe he could look at me and see me as a work in progress. Which is what we all are anyway. I don't think I'm beyond redemption. Maybe he feels the same way and can see me for my potential instead of my actual."

"Honey, that sounds great. But you know the world doesn't work that way. You're trying to wish something into being true. It just doesn't work that way." Nicki thought for a moment, then continued, "Oh, and here's another thing—

once he finds out you strip, he'll assume you turn tricks, too."

"But I *don't* turn tricks—never have, never will," Hannah said indignantly.

"But a lot of girls in the business *do*. There are girls that work right here at Polecats who do—I'm sure you must know that. Shit, I've thought about it myself. I mean, what the hell? It's just fucking."

Hannah shook her head. "I hate that word. Fucking. It's so vile, especially when it's used to refer to lovemaking."

"Lovemaking?" Nicki threw back her head and laughed. "I don't even know what that word is supposed to mean. You need to embrace this lifestyle. Make that money, honey. And when you get horny, use them the same way they use us. That's all you need a man for anyway. It would be a lot healthier for you, too. You wouldn't be rubbing yourself raw with that bar of soap because you feel dirty."

"I feel dirty because these drunk dirtballs put their hands on me. They make me feel like my skin is crawling. And the owners of this place look the other way, instead of enforcing the *no touching* rule. For three years now, I've put up with it and I'm tired of it. I'm tired of these scumbags raping me with their eyes. I've reached my breaking point. Don't these men ever think about the fact that the girls that they're ogling—and groping—are someone's sister or daughter? I mean, seriously, would they want their loved one treated that way? I almost feel like I can never be clean again."

"But you can't scrub away the past. If you embrace it, though, you won't feel guilty anymore."

Tears formed in Hannah's eyes. Her mascara ran. "We're different, Nicki. You've already given up. I haven't. One of these days, I'm going to fall in love, and that love will heal all my wounds and be the start of a new life, a new Hannah."

15

"You've seen too many old, romantic movies. And those movies were never anything more than a fantasy anyway, even in their own time. You're an idealist in a world that only rewards realists."

"I don't care, Nicki. I don't care." Hannah closed her eyes and took a deep breath. "I want to be kissed in the pouring rain."

"And I hope that wish comes true for you, baby doll. I do." Nicki finished curling her hair and applied one last coat of black lipstick before telling Hannah, "Look, I gotta go, I'm up next." Nicki put her eye patch on—she was going with the pirate costume—parted the stage curtain and walked out onto the runway. Hannah could hear the customers already carrying on. She could distinctly hear one shout to Nicki, "Yo Ho Ho and your face covered with cum!"

Hannah sat there alone. She'd have to redo her makeup before she went onstage because her tears had ruined it. But before she did that and got dressed—so she could get *undressed*—she pulled out a well-worn pink diary from her purse and opened it to a blank page and began to compose. She wrote,

Hannah's Song – Happy Endings

I want to be kissed in the pouring rain.
Holly Golightly was – I want the same.
But if I fall in love with one who will not love me.
Then . . . my Happy Ending can never be.

I want to be kissed in the pouring rain.
I want to shed a past filled with pain.
But If I fall in love with one who will not set me free.
Then . . . my Happy Ending can never be.

I want to be kissed in the pouring rain.

I want to feel the warmth of love's eternal flame.
But if I fall in love with one who, my pure soul, he cannot see.
Then . . . my Happy Ending can never be.

I want to be kissed in the pouring rain.
A life without love cannot be sustained.
But if I fall in love and our love is one-sided.
Then . . . there's no Happy Ending for a love unrequited.

She closed the diary and put it back in her purse. *It's not Shakespeare, but it's from my heart.*

"What outfit for tonight?" she muttered to herself. She selected an old standby. Naughty schoolgirl. *Can never go wrong with naughty schoolgirl—puts these perverts in touch with their inner pedophiles.* She changed into a super short black and red plaid skirt, a low-cut white top, white ankle socks with black and white saddle shoes, and a pair of black nerd glasses. She fixed her hair into pigtails and checked herself in the mirror—five-feet-six-inches and one-hundred and twenty pounds of pure sex. A gold Star of David hung from her neck. The transition to Sabrina Sinn, her stage persona, was complete.

Nicki was finishing up her set. Hannah was on next. As Nicki exited the stage, already counting her money, she told Hannah, "Break a leg, baby!"

Ronnie was the club's general manager. He was in his late 40's and had a penchant for wearing loud silk shirts, which were always generously unbuttoned to reveal thick chest hair and gold chains. He sported a bad combover and was known for his laissez-faire mentality when it came to enforcing the club's rules regarding customers putting their hands on the dancers. He doubled as the club's MC and announced Hannah to the raucous crowd.

"Okay, gents—here's what you've all been waiting for. Polecats Gentleman's Club is proud to present the woman of your dreams . . . your *wet dreams*, that is! Please put your hands together for the finest piece of ass in all of Charm City, Miss Sabrina Sinn!"

She entered to various catcalls and the sounds of The Waitresses' *I Know What Boys Like*. One guy was already screaming, "Take it off!" She skipped down the runway and began working the pole. And she was good at it. Spinning, twirling, pumping and humping it. Very athletic. A couple of minutes in, she untied her top and let it fall but covered her boobs with a hand bra. Finally, she dropped her hands and the place went nuts. She shimmied her shoulders to make her breasts shake, then held them with her hands and squeezed them. Her nipples poked through her fingers. Next, she cupped her left breast with both hands, raised it to her mouth and licked her own nipple, leaving it coated with saliva. The audience again erupted in hoots and whistles. She danced to the edge of the stage to collect the money from her adoring fans. In the front row, a middle-aged guy, balding, held up a one-hundred-dollar bill for her. He dropped the bill on the stage. She turned away from the audience and bent over at the waist. Her skirt hiked all the way up and she wasn't wearing any panties. She turned around, did a split, and leaned backward thrusting her boobs up. Finally, she got up and resumed dancing. The man who dropped the bill called her over and motioned for her to bend forward so she could hear him over the loud music.

He asked her, "Know who my favorite magician is, honey?"

"Who's that?" Hannah replied with a forced smile.

"David Cop-A-Feel!" With that, he grabbed her right breast and squeezed it.

That was it. She couldn't take it anymore. "Fucking jerk!" She kicked him in the shoulder with her saddle shoe but lost her balance and fell off the stage.

18

The customer, smarting and grabbing his shoulder, yelled, "You fucking slut! I gave you a hundred bucks. That gives me the right to grab your fucking tit if I want!" He stared at the Star of David hanging from her neck. "Well, that explains a lot. I should have known that someone with your uppity attitude was a Zionist," he said in a huff.

The bouncers finally got involved. They didn't kick the guy out because of how much money he was spending. He was a high roller, for sure, and resumed the party by taking a strap of fives and making it rain.

Hannah was helped backstage. Her left ankle was swollen already, and she couldn't put much weight on it. Nicki came to check on her. "Damn, Hannah! When I told you to break a leg, I didn't mean that literally. You need to go to the ER. It could be broken. Might even need surgery. I'll take you if you want."

"Okay, but I have to shower first."

"Honey, you couldn't even stand up in a shower right now."

"I have to shower! Now! I have to get him off of me. He's on me. He's on my skin!" She cried.

"Okay—okay—okay," Nicki told her, as she put her arm around Hannah. "Go ahead and take your shower, but you have to get that ankle checked out."

Hannah stood on her right leg in the shower that management had installed in the dressing room. She turned the knob to the left, to make the temperature as hot as she could stand. Leaning against the side of the shower for support, she scrubbed herself as hard as she could. All the while she was crying.

They got back from the ER at 4 AM. The ankle wasn't broken but was severely sprained. She'd be on crutches for a while and wouldn't be able to work for about ten days.

Nicki helped her up the front steps of Hannah's upscale Federal Hill home. They sat in her kitchen drinking coffee, as Hannah's new cat, Rain Man, clumsily attempted to bat a kibble of dry cat food around the kitchen floor. Rain Man was a disabled, two-year-old solid black cat, whom she had recently adopted from the city animal shelter.

Nicki watched as the cat staggered like a punch-drunk prizefighter. He fell over, got up, lurched forward and backward, fell over again, but doggedly pursued the elusive kibble.

Nicki asked, "What the hell is wrong with that cat? He looks like he's drunk or having a seizure or something. He doesn't have rabies, does he?"

"Oh, God. No! He does *not* have rabies! He has Cerebellar Hypoplasia, CH. It means that he's a little unsteady on his feet, that's all. He was born that way. But he's not in any pain and it's not a progressive disease. He doesn't even realize he's different from other cats."

Nicki shook her head. "Didn't they have any normal cats?"

Indignantly, Hannah said, "Maybe I didn't want a normal one. The normal ones are always more likely to get adopted. He already had two strikes against him—his disability and the fact that he's all black. The shelter staff said the all-black cats always have a harder time finding homes."

"What's up with his name—Rain Man?"

"That was the name he was given at the shelter because he had been dumped outside their gate one morning in pouring down rain. It just kind of stuck. It seemed to fit him, so I kept it . . . pick him up and hand him to me, will you?" Nicki awkwardly picked up the cat and passed him off to Hannah. She cradled him like a baby. "And momma loves her little man, doesn't she?" she asked the cat as she kissed his forehead.

"You mind if I smoke?" Nicki asked.

"Right here in the house? Yes. I do." Hannah motioned towards the cat. "Baby doesn't need to inhale your second-hand smoke. Let's go out on the porch."

Hannah put Rain Man down and clumsily propelled herself on her crutches. She had never been on crutches before and was still getting the hang of it.

They went out onto the front porch and each lit up a Virginia Slims cigarette and shivered in the predawn chill.

Hannah shook her head. "That guy tonight! What a fucking creep. I'll never forget him, never forget his face. Such an air of entitlement. Like *oh, I gave you a hundred bucks, now I can do anything I want to you.* Asshole! He's an anti-Semite, too. He said something about my Star of David. Once he saw it, he was, like *oh yeah, I guess that explains how you act.*"

Nicki nodded. "I know a lot of the guys who come into the club are jerks, but look on the bright side, you got yourself a ten days' paid vacation, girl. What are you going to do with that time? Are you still going to keep your date with Mr. Wonderful? Are you going to tell him you hurt yourself kicking a creepy middle-aged pervert who was trying to fondle your bodacious ta-tas after you shook your money-maker for him at a strip club? Hmm?"

Hannah was happy to have the time off, happy to be free from the stress of Polecats for a while.

"I'm definitely going to keep the date and there are a million ways to hurt your ankle, so I can come up with an explanation."

Nicki wagged her finger at her and sarcastically said, "Tisk! Tisk! Starting a relationship off with a lie is like building a house on a faulty foundation. At least that's what Dr. Phil says."

"Yeah? Well, Dr. Phil also tells people *never waste a good chance to shut up.* So there." She stuck her tongue out at

Nicki.

They finished their smokes and Nicki prepared to leave. "Look, I'm going to head home and get some sleep." She started to walk towards her new BMW and after a few steps, turned and said, "You know, I really do hope this guy is a Mister Wonderful." She winked at Hannah.

Hannah nodded. "Thanks."

Nicki beeped her horn as she pulled out and Hannah waved to her.

Then she went inside and laid down on the couch with a bag of buttered popcorn. Rain Man jumped up with her and sat on her chest. She turned on the TV and tuned in to the network that only showed classic movies. They were playing some old Jimmy Stewart romantic comedy. She closed her eyes and imagined herself as his leading lady. Then she and Rain Man fell asleep.

CHAPTER FOUR: LUNCH AT TIFFANY'S

David sat outside Tiffany's Diner on Loch Raven Boulevard in his vintage black Lincoln Town Car with the window slightly cracked, listening to sports talk radio and smoking a cigarette. He got caught up at the Coffee Hour social following the ten o'clock service and didn't have time to change, so underneath his black windbreaker, he was wearing his black clerical shirt and a white Roman collar. He wore matching black pants, oxfords, and belt. A smart looking black fedora topped off his wardrobe. He looked at his watch. It was five after twelve. *Wonder if she's even going to show.*

A few minutes later, a late model red SUV pulled in and parked right next to him. It had a bumper sticker that read *Animals – It's Their World Too.* Hannah got out with her crutches.

As he got out of the vehicle, he called out, "What happened to you?"

She smiled. "Oh, it's nothing. A little accident at work on Friday night, that's all. It's not broken, just badly sprained."

"What happened?"

"You know, little old clumsy me. I fell and came down the wrong way. Sorry I'm late, but I forgot my laptop, so I went home to get it. I know you said you'd bring legal pads, but I can type a lot faster than I can write."

"Are you in much pain?"

"A little. Not too bad, though. I took some ibuprofen right before I left the house and that helps some. But I'm going to

23

be off work for a while, so I guess you're not the only one who's on vacation." He felt relief that he hadn't been stood up.

She was wearing a white fisherman's sweater and blue jeans, a white canvass sneaker on her right foot and a pink sock and ankle brace on her left foot. Her hair was down. And her bar of soap dangled from her wrist. He caught a whiff of her perfume and recognized it as Philosophy's *Falling In Love.*

"Do you need any help?"

"Oh, no, no. I'm fine. I'm getting the hang of these crutches."

Tiffany's. An old-time, 1950s style diner complete with a jukebox that played only oldies. It catered to a working-class clientele and served breakfast twenty-four hours a day. The place was decked out in lots of pink and white Formica, and the walls were decorated with vintage Baltimore sports memorabilia. Pennants, autographed photos, framed jerseys and the like.

As soon as they walked in, he smelled burgers and pancakes cooking on the grill and fresh coffee brewing.

They walked past a booth full of middle-aged blue-collar workers who were all still wearing their orange hard hats and brown tool belts. David thought that they probably worked in the Sparrows Point steel mills. As they ate their breakfast, they debated which was the better band, Styx or Cheap Trick. One of them cast his vote by walking over to the juke box and playing *The Best of Times.*

Hannah bobbed her head and mouthed the words to the song as they scanned the room, looking for a good place to sit. "I love this song," she casually noted as she continued to survey the dining area.

Finally, David pointed to a small table in the middle of the diner. She nodded. They walked over, and he pulled out the chair for her and she gingerly sat down.

She smiled. "Only two men have ever done that for me," she said. "My dad and my uncle, so you're in good company. Thank you. That made me feel good." She laid her crutches down across an adjacent empty booth.

He nodded. "My pleasure." Then he added, "You know, that's a nice little SUV you have there."

"Thanks. It gets decent mileage and it cuts right through the snow. That's mainly why I got it. And you drive—what was that?"

"A nineteen ninety-seven Town Car, Signature Series."

"Right. Yeah. I thought it was a Lincoln."

He leaned forward and whispered, "You know why I drive a big car like that?"

She shook her head.

"So when Pauly orders me to whack somebody, I have plenty of room in the trunk for the body." He looked at her with a total poker face.

"Pauly?"

"Psych!" He howled, pleased with himself.

She reached over and playfully smacked his hand. "That was mean."

He laughed harder and took off his windbreaker and fedora. He could see the shock on her face when she saw the Roman collar. He knew it was coming.

"What's wrong, Hannah?"

"You're . . . you're . . . you're a priest? You're a priest?"

"Whoa. Hold on."

"You're a priest!"

"Oh, no, no, no. You've got it all wrong. I am an ordained minister, but I'm not Catholic. I'm Protestant. Anglican to be exact. It's kind of Catholic lite."

"So . . . that means . . . what?" She looked at him with suspicion,

He chuckled. "That we're good. You know, you and me."

He pointed at her and then himself. "We're good to be here together." This conversation was always awkward. He regrouped. "It means I can sit here and have lunch with a pretty woman without risking eternal damnation."

"So you're allowed to . . . you know, do this type of thing? In other words, you're allowed to hang out with women? Gosh, that sounded so clumsy, didn't it?"

"No. You're not clumsy. It's just a clumsy topic in general, that's all. And yeah, I'm totally allowed to hang out with women. I guess maybe I should have told you when we talked at the zoo that I'm a member of the clergy."

"No—no. You're good, you're fine."

"I didn't want to scare you off."

"Scare me off?"

"Yes. Sometimes, it can be tough for members of the clergy to make connections. People don't want to hang around us because they assume we'll judge them or won't be much fun to be around because we're so prudish. That type of thing. The reality is that we're human, too. We want the same things that anyone else would want in life. And we make mistakes. I'm not perfect."

"I'm not perfect, either."

"Then maybe we can be imperfect together. Besides, perfection's pretty damn boring if you ask me."

She smiled. "I'm just relieved that you don't work for a guy named *Pauly*."

Madge, the waitress, came over to take their orders. She looked like she had been sent in by Central Casting to play the role. 60ish, she chewed gum, wore too much makeup, smelled of cheap perfume, and had a hairstyle that went out of fashion with Nehru jackets. Hannah and David both ordered *the usual*. Madge smiled, popped her gum, and shook her head. "Okay, two egg salad sandwiches on rye with lettuce and tomato, a side order of onion rings, and two orange sodas comin' right up." She picked up the menus and walked back to the kitchen.

"Wow. You're an egg salad fan, too?" Hannah asked.

"Yeah. Egg is the forgotten salad if you think about it. I mean, every diner has tuna salad, chicken salad. Some even have crab and shrimp salad. But not many have egg salad anymore. Egg salad is the victim of culinary discrimination."

"So maybe we can add that to our list of crusades. Help the caged lions and bring egg salad back from its unjust egg-cile."

"Egg-actly." He nodded. *She's witty, good sense of humor. I don't get the whole soap-on-a-rope thing, but if a bulky good-luck charm is her biggest idiosyncrasy, I can live with that.*

While they were waiting for the food, they got down to business. Hannah opened her laptop and David pulled a small legal pad out of his jacket pocket.

Hannah began typing. "So how about if we call this project *Operation Freedom*? That's what we're after, right? Freedom. Freedom for Bobby and Babs."

"I like it. I think social media will be key. We should set up a Facebook page called *Free Bobby and Babs*. Oh, and I also have a contact down at WJZ TV. He'd probably be willing to do a story about Colonel Rupert's operation." He wrote on his legal pad as Hannah typed.

"Letters to the editor, too. People do still read the paper, even if it's only the digital version. I could write a letter to the editor of *The Baltimore Sun*. I like writing," she said.

"I'll write one, too. The more, the better." There was a brief pause, then he smiled. "So you're a writer, are you?"

"I didn't say that. I mean, I've never been published."

"Doesn't matter. A writer is *one who writes* . . . right?"

"I don't even do that yet."

"What type of writing are you interested in?"

"Fiction. Novels. I was an English major at the University of Maryland."

"What kind of novels do you want to write?"

She looked down and fiddled with a napkin. "You won't laugh?"

"Of course not."

"Well, I *don't* want to write those mindless bodice rippers that you see in the drugstores. I want to write a real novel, one that says something important about life, you know? I want to make people think and feel. I want to make them laugh on one page and cry on the next. I want to move them. All good writers have that ability. To move people with words on a page."

"Who's your favorite writer?"

She looked up and deeply exhaled. "Tough one. But if I can only pick one, I'd say Truman Capote."

"Why Capote?"

"Because he wrote so simply. No fancy, Ivy League words. He knew that it's the simple words, in the right order, strategically placed in a story — that's what moves people. He knew how to stay out of his own way, too. And he reads like a voice in your head. His stuff reads so well aloud. It's nice that way."

He nodded agreement. *Smart is sexy.*

"Speaking of Capote, we're one meal away from one of his more famous works," he said, wanting to show that he could be witty, too.

"One meal away?" She thought for a moment. "Oh. Oh! I get it! We're having *lunch at Tiffany's*. Very clever, padre. *Breakfast at Tiffany's* — that was a good little novella, but, honestly, I liked the movie better. The film had a happier ending. When she finds the cat at the end and they kiss in the downpour, with the soaked cat in between them . . . oh, my God. It gets to me every time. I tear up just thinking about it. If that scene doesn't touch your very soul, then you don't have one."

"I agree. For all us sappy romantics, the film was much more satisfying. And you know, I've always thought that the cat was a symbol. She's at her most vulnerable in that final scene and when she finds the cat, she finally finds herself."

"Yes! I've always thought that, too. Exactly. The beautiful irony is that the thing she's most afraid of is the one thing that can set her free. When she finds Cat, she realizes that. Oh, so sweet and gentle. A beautiful, lovely story."

"So do you have any beautiful, lovely stories like that in you, yet?" he asked.

She looked down, shook her head and fiddled with silverware on the table. "Not just yet. I'm waiting for inspiration."

"Don't wait for it to find you. Find *it*."

"It's not that easy. I mean, you're creating something out of nothing when you write. That's not terribly easy."

"You have to set your mind to it. Just decide, *I'm going to be a writer.*"

"I wish I *could* be a writer. God knows I hate my job."

"What kind of work do you do?"

"Oh, I . . . ah . . . I work in the . . . hospitality industry."

"You mean like hotels, restaurants, that type of thing?"

She emphatically nodded and pointed at him with her index finger. "Yup. Exactly."

"Well, which one?"

"The place I work, it serves, you know, it serves alcohol and some food. And there's live entertainment every night."

"So like a nightclub?"

"Yeah. A nightclub. It's a club that's open at night. Yep."

"What's the name of the place?"

She briefly hesitated. "That's the thing. It's just called The Club. That's our whole hook—you know, such a basic name. Everyone else is trying to be clever and complex and we went in the opposite direction. Basic, simple. It's like being unoriginal makes you original. Being boring is actually exciting. Like that rock group that just called itself *The Band*."

"Never heard of *The Club*. Is it around here?"

"No. It's not in Baltimore. It's well outside of the city. It's owned by a parent company—a company called, um . . . T&A Hospitality Services."

"What do you do there?"

"A hostess."

"Cool. Maybe once your ankle heals and you go back to work, I'll drop by some night. I'd love to see you in action. I'm sure you do an amazing job."

She looked down and nervously fiddled with a salt shaker, tilting it and spinning it like a top. "Ah-ha. Amazing. I do an amazing job."

Madge brought out their food.

Excitedly, she called out, "Food's here! Enough shop talk. Let's eat."

He looked at the two plates of food that were identical. "The bad thing about two people having the same taste is that it's not as much fun stealing from the other person's plate," he said.

"Oh, so you're one of *those* types, eh?" She leaned forward, smiled, and twirled her hair around her finger.

"Yup. I like to employ the old distract and snatch technique. I create a diversion first, see? So I'd be, like *look, Hannah! That guy behind you has a sweat stain that looks like Elvis.* And when you turn to look, I'd swipe some of your fries."

"You're funny."

He channeled Tommy from *Goodfellas*. "So you think I'm *funny*? What do you mean by that? *I'm funny.* What, like, I'm here to be your own personal frickin court jester or something? Funny like that? Like I'm some big *joke* to you, lady, is that it?" He grinned, proud of his spot-on impression.

She laughed so hard orange soda came out of her nose.

Her eyes were watering.

"Oh, God! That soda just burned my nose. I hate when that happens!" She paused as she recovered.

"You okay?" he asked. He pulled out another travel sized pack of tissues and offered it to her.

She waved him off. "Oh, thanks but I'm good." She started to laugh again. "It's just that you sounded exactly like him. I hated that character. I was so glad when he got whacked. I know it's awful to say that, but it's true." She steered the conversation back to the lions. "Getting back to Bobby and Babs—we should contact the Finally Free Foundation. I can take care of that."

"Yeah. I've heard of them. They're the ones who try to get exotic animals out of circuses and roadside zoos and back into the wild. That's a wonderful idea."

"Do you think we have a chance to make this happen?" she asked.

He nodded and emphatically said, "Absolutely."

She looked him in the eye and said, "If those two, who have been caged their entire lives, can be set free, then freedom's possible for anyone, right?"

He again nodded. "Sure."

Still looking him in the eye, she said, "I'm Jewish." She pulled out the gold Star of David pendant from underneath her sweater and displayed it to him.

"And?"

"You don't care?"

"Nope. That's a lovely pendant though," he said as he casually took a big bite of his sandwich. He pointed to her plate and with a mouthful of egg salad asked, "You gonna eat that pickle?"

"Oh, ah, no, no. Knock yourself out." He took her pickle.

"Now, getting back to the discussion of faith—" she pressed.

He interrupted, "—I love *Faith*. My favorite George Michael song, God rest his soul."

She deeply exhaled. "*Come on*. I'm trying to be serious. This isn't funny. I don't want my religion to cause problems for you. I mean, there might still be people, even in the twenty-first century, who would object to a Christian minister and a Jewish girl hanging out."

He finally turned serious. "And what if there are? Are we going to let their bigotry take away our freedom? You let me worry about that stuff, okay?"

She tentatively nodded.

He raised his eyebrows and asked again, "*Okay?*"

"Okay. Okay." She smiled as she picked up a tin of Old Bay seasoning and sprinkled it over her onion rings and then dunked one of the rings in catsup. "Do you like being a minister or reverend or whatever the right title is?"

He gave her a hard look. "That's a tough question to answer. It's definitely not what I thought it would be. I love helping people, but there's a lot of things about it I don't care for. Plus, my first love is baseball. It's a huge part of my life. I played at Sewanee University, in Tennessee, and was pretty darn good. Good enough to get drafted by Cincinnati in the tenth round as a pitcher. They even gave me a fifty-thousand dollar signing bonus because I'm left-handed. I'm proud to say that I banked it into a money market account and have never touched it. I'm saving it for a rainy day." He hesitated. *Damn! Why did I mention money? Now she's going to think that I'm a materialistic braggart. I just made myself sound like Waldo from The Little Rascals. Oh, well, too late now.* He took a deep breath and continued with the story. "But then the Reds organization turned right around and traded me to Baltimore. During my second season in Class A ball at Bel Air, I tore my rotator cuff and my career was over before it began. I never had a chance to get to the big leagues." He opened his wallet and showed her his minor league baseball card. "Here. See?"

She took the card and giggled as she read the front of the card aloud. "Let's see here . . . *Bud O'Malley, left-handed pitcher, Bel Air Bay Cats.* Bud?"

"Yeah. Bud was my baseball nickname. Long story."

"Hey, I'm off work for the next ten days. I've nothing but time." She leaned forward and smiled.

"Okay. Well, I already told you Cincinnati drafted me and then traded me. So when the Orioles called Cincy about acquiring me, they offered one hundred thousand dollars cash. See, in baseball, players can get traded strictly for money. But the Reds said that wasn't enough. So the Orioles said *all right, we'll give you one hundred grand plus twenty cases of Budweiser.* When the Reds got that counteroffer, they said *done!* After that, I was *Bud* for the rest of my playing days."

"I'm calling bullshit on that."

"It most certainly is not," he said indignantly. "I can show you the paperwork. In the trade agreement, it literally mentions the beer."

"Oh my God! Seriously?" He emphatically nodded. She shook her head. "That's, like, so freaking crazy."

"I know, right?"

She made a sad face and told him. "Guess you didn't even merit a good, imported beer, huh?"

"The people who were going to be the beneficiaries of that part of the deal weren't imported beer types," he said.

"Did you chew tobacco? You have nice teeth, a nice smile, so I'm guessing you stayed away from that stuff. It's disgusting." She made a face.

"I tried it once but discovered that I had bit off more than I could chew."

"Boo! Hiss!"

"Go right ahead and boo me. Wouldn't be the first time my baseball career caused me to be booed."

She shook her head in disgust but had a big smile on her

face. "Okay, back to the card. Let's turn it over and see what the back says." Again, she read from the card, "*Fun fact — In his spare time, Bud enjoys watching soap operas.* Soap operas? Really?" She laughed and teasingly asked, "Want to come over to my place tomorrow afternoon and we can split a box of tissues while we watch *The High and The Mighty?* Blair has amnesia again and she forgot that she's in love with Blake and is about to marry the handsome and rich but supremely evil Lionel Barrington, who kidnapped Blair's mother to prevent her from stopping the ceremony. What Lionel doesn't know, however, is that Blair's mother is a witch and she's conjuring up a spell to turn him into a lawn gnome."

He snatched the card from her hand. "Hardy har har. So now you know one of my guilty pleasures. But I'm confident enough in my masculinity that I can admit that — yes — I'm captivated by the drama, passion, and intrigue of the soaps. Okay?"

"Hey, no judgment here." She again snickered, then raised her eyebrows. "And I know another one of your guilty pleasures."

"You do, do you? Well, come on, lay it on me, sister."

She smiled an ornery smile and blurted out, "You, sir, go to a tanning salon! Dun, Dun, Dun! Busted!"

"Maybe I got this healthy, rich color on vacation."

"Oh, you just started your vacation and, besides, you'd have to be vacationing on the surface of the freaking sun it-self to get that dark. That's a *Jersey Shore* tan, honey." She stuck her tongue out at him and blew raspberries.

He laughed. "Okay. Guilty as charged. So there — now you know. I'm a little vain . . . maybe."

"I mean, it looks okay, don't get me wrong. It's just a bit much. If it were subtler, it would look amazing," she said.

"Yeah, well, I never intended to get this dark. I actually haven't been tanning in about two weeks. This is all from my last visit. I, ah, I got overcooked."

"Got overcooked?"

"Yeah, I told the salon attendant that I wanted *fifteen minutes in a Level 1 Bed* and she thought I said *fifty minutes.* And I never noticed because I fell asleep. It's very relaxing in those tanning beds, you see, and they were piping in some Burt Bacharach to boot. It's actually faded a good bit now."

She shook her head as she laughed. "That's quite a story there, fella. I would have hated to see what you looked like right afterward."

"For the first few hours I was radioactive."

She laughed again, shook her head, and picked up a napkin. "Here. You've got some egg salad on your face. Let me get that for you. And I'm just giving you a hard time. It's kind of cute. It shows you're human, since vanity is a very human quality."

"Exactly. It only makes me more endearing. One year I even participated in the Tanning Olympics?"

"Tanning Olympics?"

"Yep. I took home the bronze. *Ba dum ching.*" He imitated a drum roll and cymbal crash.

She took the napkin and threw it at him. "Oh, that's awful. Hopefully, telling bad jokes like that one will help keep that vanity of yours in check. You definitely don't have a future in stand-up comedy."

Then she turned serious. "So you'd rather be a ballplayer than a minister?"

"It's a moot point because I'm a twenty-eight-year-old with a torn rotator cuff. Sometimes, I think that I'd like to be a baseball announcer, though. When I was a kid, I used to listen to Vin Scully calling ball games for NBC. And it was like he was an old friend who was coming into your house to describe the action and keep you company. I was an only child and very shy. Didn't have many friends. But I always felt that Vin Scully was my friend. I kind of think that I'd like to bring that feeling to others. But I do feel called by God to serve the Church." He shrugged his shoulders. "Like a lot of things in life, it's complicated, I guess."

"What don't you like about being a minister?"

"Well, you get into it thinking that it's all about helping people, but you quickly find out that the church can be every bit as political, petty, and mean-spirited as the rest of the world. In some ways, it's like working for any other big corporation. All these rules, and policies, and directives . . ." He shook his head, then continued, "They prevent you from helping the people who really need help. And then there's the hypocrisy. You have to deal with people who claim sainthood for themselves but are some of the worst sinners you'll ever meet. I'm kind of burned out on it, to be honest. I swear — sometimes I feel like this Roman collar that I wear is like the collar my dog wears, except her collar only has a leash attached when we go for a walk. But this collar" — he took his hand and tugged on his Roman collar before continuing — "this collar always has a leash attached. And a very short one, at that. That's why I'm glad I'm on vacation."

"So go to broadcasting school and become a baseball announcer. Become the next Vin Scully."

"I'll do that as soon as you quit your job to become a writer. And the next Truman Capote."

She turned serious. "I'm not trying to be the next Truman Capote. I'm trying to be the first Hannah Cohen." He nodded approvingly. *Touché.*

There was a brief pause.

"You know, I like baseball, too," she said.

"Yeah?"

"Yeah. Huge O's fan. I was always a tomboy growing up. Loved playing and watching sports. I played both field hockey and softball at the University of Maryland."

He raised his eyebrows. "Tomboys are *sexy*. Nothing sexier than a girl who can hit a curveball."

She tilted her head and softly bit her lower lip. "You wouldn't be trying to throw *me* a curve now, would you?"

"Me? Never. But I think if I did, you'd hit it out of the park." He paused. "Can I tell you something else?"

"Go on."

"You're awfully pretty."

She blushed and looked down. "And you're awfully sweet. Thank you. You sure know how to make a woman feel special."

"You *are* special, Hannah. I'm calling attention to the obvious, that's all."

She looked up, looked him directly in the eye. "Sometimes that's what people need." She briefly put her hand under her chin and then pointed at him. "You know, you remind me of my uncle, Uncle Oskar. He was so funny, and sweet, and kind, and decent. Oh, everybody loved Uncle Oskar. *Everybody*. Oskar Schindler Cohen. That name was a tribute because my great-grandmother was on the list. You know, *The* list. I guess I'm here today because of Oskar Schindler."

"There. You see. One person can make all the difference, like I was telling you."

"I've often wondered — what made him do it? He had nothing to gain and everything to lose. Did he have some type of secret death wish?" she asked.

He adamantly shook his head. "Not a death wish. A life wish. Amid all that *inhumanity*, he found *humanity* deep within himself, in his own personal holy of holies. He became an angel in the devil's den. He brought a little piece of Heaven to a hellish time and place. And he found his own freedom by freeing others."

She nodded and looked down again. "The way you said

that—that was almost poetic. You have a way with words. I imagine you must preach a good sermon." She smiled a weak smile before continuing, "You know, there's a nice story about Uncle Oskar, one that makes me very proud. He once went into a convenience store in Manhattan—he lived in New York—and picked up a case of water and accidentally forgot to pay for it. He was in a terrible hurry that day. But as he walked out the door, he turned around and pulled out a twenty-dollar bill and put it on the counter and told the store manager to keep the change. Then thanked him for not being angry about him almost walking out without paying. That's a wonderful story. It makes me cry sometimes when I think of it."

He was underwhelmed. "It makes you cry that he paid for his merchandise?"

She nodded and looked up. "Yes. He was a New York City firefighter. And he took the case of water for his buddies and civilians who were injured on the morning of September eleventh." Her voice cracked. "But he still wanted to pay for it, you know? And there is something so magnificent in that. A magnificent nobility. That in the midst of all that horror and chaos, he still wanted to make sure he gave the man the money for the water, even though that was the last thing on the manager's mind at that point. That's special."

He wasn't sure if he should ask. After a few silent seconds, he said, "Did, um, did he make it out?"

She shook her head. "He was in the North Tower when it collapsed. And he was a hero. A real hero, not one of these fake heroes that our society loves to create and celebrate. When he walked into that tower on that beautiful September morning, he knew he was walking into Hell. And he never once hesitated. We've talked about freedom . . . well, my uncle died literally trying to set people free, people he didn't even know. That's the best you can do. To give the gift of freedom without asking for anything in return."

He didn't know what to say. Despite all his seminary training in counseling people, he never knew quite what to say when it was his turn to talk during these types of conversations. *There's never any magic words that will make someone's pain go away and the worst thing you can do is be trite and patronizing.*

He reached out and patted her hand. "This is the part where I guess I'm supposed to say something deep and profound. But I can't do that because you already have, and there's no way for me to top that. You see, you have a way with words, too, Hannah Cohen. So I'll simply say . . . I'm sorry."

"You're sweet." She nodded, pushed some food around on her plate with her fork, and repeated herself. "You're sweet, you are."

He tried to lighten the mood a bit. He cleared his throat. "You want to go to the Orioles game tomorrow with me? Yankees are in town. I have two tickets. The seats are right behind the Yankees' dugout, so we can heckle them."

"Yeah! I'd love that. I can't stand those Yankees, those damn Yankees," she said.

"What Oriole fan can? In fact, who outside of the Bronx can?" he asked.

She curled both of her tiny hands into fists and shook them emphatically, looked upwards and clenched her teeth. "Oh, and that new rookie sensation that the Yankees have, that Bam-Bam Bradford. He's so smug. The way he blows kisses to taunt the other team's fans when he hits a home run. No class. And he's not that great if you ask me. He sits on fastballs. If you throw him a good change-up or slider, you can freeze him up."

Damn. This woman knows baseball. "Can I pick you up around six?"

"Yeah. Sure." She wrote her address down for him and he

glanced at it

"Federal Hill, huh? Swanky."

"Well, where do you live?" she asked.

"Guilford."

"Oh, that's old money, honey. Much more upscale than The Hill."

"Yeah, but it's a house owned by the Diocese."

He got up and walked over to the jukebox and perused the selections and went back to the table, telling her, "Couldn't find the one I was looking for." So he pulled out his phone and found it.

"I'd like to dedicate this song to Bobby and Babs and their impending freedom. Cheers," he said.

They raised their glasses of orange soda and clinked them together.

He turned up the volume and began to play John Barry's version of *Born Free*.

"Dance with me, Hannah. Please."

"I can't dance." She pointed to her left ankle. "Remember?"

He smacked himself in the forehead. "Oh, yeah. Duh! I actually forgot." He thought for a moment and snapped his fingers. "Let's try something. Stand up on your crutches for a sec."

"What?" She looked at him with mild suspicion.

"Indulge me here. Might not work. But I promise I won't hurt you." She gingerly stood up and he put his arms around her waist and gently lifted her a couple of inches off the ground. She set her crutches down.

"Does that hurt at all?"

"Uh-uh. My legs aren't even touching the ground."

"All right, then we are going to have our dance. I'll keep you lifted off the ground." He held her up with one strong arm and, with his free hand, gently brushed her hair.

She wrapped her legs around his, so they wouldn't swing.

"I promise to never hurt you," he said.

She looked him in the eye and nodded. "I'll hold you to that." Then, she smiled and asked, "So we're going to slow dance right here in the diner?"

"Sure."

"But what will everyone think?"

"Maybe they'll look at us and think — *those two people over there . . . they're free enough that they don't care what we think.*"

Once he said that he thought he saw a tear in her eye. He held her up very close and danced for the both of them. She put her arms around him, closed her eyes and buried her face in his shoulder. He felt her breasts pressing against his chest, heard her sniffle, smelled the jasmine and vanilla of her perfume mixed with the *fresh linen* smell of her fabric softener, and saw her shiny blonde hair as he held her. He felt a warmth, both literal and figurative, radiating from her body. And it felt good – *so* good.

The diner got quiet, so quiet that the sounds of dishes being clanked against one another as they were washed in the back of the house could be heard. Some customers stopped eating and talking and just watched in silence. When it was over, several people stood and applauded. Hannah blew kisses to their audience, smiled, and gave them the beauty pageant wave. David blushed.

As they were leaving, a young woman, about eighteen, stopped them. She had used her phone to take a video of them dancing and wanted their permission to post it on social media.

He looked at Hannah. "Okay with me so long as it's okay with you."

Hannah shrugged her shoulders and nodded. "Sure. Fine with me."

The young woman gave them her YouTube channel information. Her channel was called *Tell Me Something Good* and contained only uplifting, feel-good videos. Within minutes, the video was up and getting views under the title, *"Chivalry is not dead! "Reverend Romance" Literally Sweeps Woman Off Her Feet in Baltimore Diner!*

CHAPTER FIVE: VIRAL

On Monday, Hannah sprawled out on her bed, opened her laptop, and started to organize her thoughts for her letter to the editor. Rain Man lay next to her, sleeping and snoring loudly.

The doorbell rang, and Hannah rolled her eyes. *I just got comfortable.* Getting up and down the stairs in her two-story brick townhome proved difficult with her injury. Via trial and error, she found that the easiest way was to sit on the steps and either pull herself up or push herself down, all the while keeping her left leg completely extended. It worked but took a long time. The doorbell continued to ring with someone's impatience. *Damn! Give me a chance, will you?* When she opened the door, Nicki was standing there, wearing very tight-fitting jeans and a tight t-shirt. No bra. The t-shirt was decorated with a cartoon of a very well-endowed woman. Below the caricature were the words, *Got Milk?*

"Hey, girl. I was out shopping before I head into work and I picked up one of those pain patches for you. Don't worry, it's not Fentanyl or anything. Strictly OTC. I know I owe you ten bucks anyway, so you can deduct that from my debt. Got time for a smoke?"

"Sure." *I would rather have the cash.*

They went to the front porch. Nicki passed Hannah one of her cigarettes and they lit up.

Nicki took a deep drag and exhaled. "So I bet you know the real reason I dropped by, huh?"

"You're a busybody."

"Honey, my body is always busy, if you know what I mean."

"I meant you were nosy about how my lunch with David went."

"Well, since *you're* the one who brought it up, I guess we can talk about it if you really want."

Hannah pulled her phone from the front pocket of her pink sweatpants and held it up for Nicki to view. "Here. Check out this video." She was proud to show off the clip.

Nicki watched with her mouth open. "Oh, my God. This was just yesterday, and it's got over one-hundred thousand views already. You all went viral, girl! You can't see your face that good though because you have it buried in his shoulder. Good view of that sweet little ass of yours though. Oh, and your guy is adorable. I'd fuck him."

"*Beg your pardon?*" Hannah understood that it was Nicki's nature to tease, but was nonetheless offended by the comment.

"Retract your claws, baby doll. I'm speaking hypothetically. Like, if you weren't so into him, well, then, what the hell, I'd fuck him. I mean, if he came into Polecats, I'd take him home and fuck him. No big deal."

"He would never be in Polecats," Hannah insisted.

"Oh, how do you know? You certainly don't know everything there is to know about him."

"Your problem, Nicki, is that you don't realize that for some people sex isn't an end unto itself, but a means to an end. In other words, love is the true end. Sex is a way to express that love."

Nicki threw up her hands. "*What. Eveeer.* But like I said, I'd never mess with anyone you like. No man is worth it. So relax, tiger, I'm not trying to steal your man. He is cute though."

"That's good because this little tigress is *very* territorial."

Hannah playfully hissed at Nicki and held her fingers up to imitate claws. They both laughed, but Hannah was only half-joking.

"You tell him you're a stripper?"

"I told him I work in a club, which isn't exactly a lie."

"But you didn't tell him it's a strip club?"

"No, and please spare me Dr. Phil's advice. I don't want to hear it."

"Fine. Fine." Nicki grinned a shit-eating grin and turned to another topic. "You don't have to answer, but have you done the old *Boom-Boom* yet?" Nicki thrust her pelvis forward.

"We've only been on one date, which technically wasn't even a date. It was a brainstorming session. We haven't even kissed yet."

Nicki shook her head. "No—no—no—no. No! You've been on *two* dates." She held up two fingers in Hannah's face. "The zoo thing counted as a date and so did lunch. Two dates. You know what that means? Three Date Rule, girl! So next time you see him, it'll be time to feed the kitty. Unless, of course, he's gay."

"Okay, well, first, the zoo thing was *not* a date. Okay? Second, there is no Three Date Rule. Now, there is a rule that if you're in a long line at the supermarket and they open a new checkout lane, the person who's been waiting the longest has the right of first refusal. Yes! That is a rule and I hate when people don't observe it. But there is no Three Date Rule. It's a very personal matter, and I'm not going to let some nonexistent *rule* govern me. And he's not gay. So stop trying to fill my mind with nonexistent roadblocks."

"All I'm saying is that your gaydar has never worked properly. You fell for that gay guy . . . what was his name . . . Charles? You know, the guy you met at the library about a year ago. Remember? You thought he was your new BF and he thought you were his new BFF. And even when he told you that his dream vacation was a week at a dude ranch, you still didn't get it. In fact, you had no idea you were barking up the wrong tree until you mentioned that you had a celebrity crush on Bradley Cooper and he was, like *yeah me, too.* Remember? Hmm?"

"I knew you were going to dredge that up. So I was wrong one time. So what?"

"Maybe you should give this David a test, a gay test."

"A *gay* test?"

"Sure. Give him a lap dance. Grind on him. I mean really grind on him, and if he pulls a Shania Twain and is all, like *honey, that don't impress me much,* then you know it's a lost cause. On the other hand, if you succeed in rousing his soldier to stand at attention for you, you'll know you're on solid ground. After all, with men, it's always been the same." Nicki pointed to the area between her thighs with her index finger and continued, "They get kicked out of there at birth and literally spend the rest of their lives trying to get back in. And why shouldn't they? When they were in there before, they had a woman to do everything for them. I swear—if they could shrink themselves into tiny little men and put a tiny TV set in there that got ESPN and a tiny fridge stocked with tiny cold cuts and tiny bottles of beer, they'd never come out. They'd just chill the fuck out in there forever."

Hannah rolled her eyes. "You're impossible. I'm not going to give him a *gay test.* I would never do that. And I'm not rushing into anything. I like this guy. I'm going to take things as they come and see where they lead."

"Yeah, well it would probably get a little awkward for you to have sex now because of your ankle. No way you could be on top. You guys would have to go with good old-fashioned missionary." Nicki did a fake and exaggerated yawn. "Bor-ing."

"Please don't tell me how or when to have sex. And speaking of missionary, did you happen to notice what David was wearing in the video?"

Nicki squinted her eyes and looked closer. "All black. What's he Goth or something?"

"He's an ordained minister." Hannah crossed her arms and took a deep drag on her cigarette.

Nicki threw her head back and cackled. "Oh, shit! Hannah's falling in love with a freaking minister! I can see the tabloid headlines now — *The Saint and the Sinner*. I'll go ahead and book you two on all those trashy day-time talk shows. Maybe there could even be a movie. The film version could use your stage name. You know, *The Saint and Miss Sinn*. Sounds like the title of a nineteen seventies skin flick."

"Stop laughing at me." Hannah flashed a scowl.

"Honey, I'm sorry, but this can't end well. You know that. End it before it even begins so you don't get hurt." Nicki smoked her cigarette down to the filter, started with her smoker's cough, and threw the butt in a tin coffee can filled with sand that was sitting on the porch.

"He won't hurt me. He promised he'd never hurt me."

"So a guy promises you something and you believe him?"

"I think this one's different."

"You're never going to learn. Never. It's sad."

"What's sad is that you can't find enough hope to believe that there's still some good out there." Hannah continued to speak, but she stared straight ahead, and her eyes got a faraway look. "He treated me like I matter, made me feel important. He was interested in my dreams. He looked me in the eyes, not in the boobs. He made me feel like a human being, instead of a piece of meat." Hannah came out of her trance and looked at Nicki, telling her, "And you know, Nicki, in your heart of hearts — you know — that you crave those same things. But it's easier for you to deny that they exist than to take a chance on them. Because then you might get hurt. You play it off like you're the tough one and I'm this weak, stupid little waif. But you're not tough. You're not even tough enough to believe in love and, trust me, it takes some toughness to believe in it. But you can't or won't, so you're already condemned to be lonely and miserable."

Nicki briefly stared at her and the two women looked at one another in silence. Finally, Nicki shook her head in disgust and said, "Look, I have to go. Gotta go to work." Hannah threw down her cigarette butt and watched Nicki as she got into her BMW. When she maneuvered her way back inside and into the kitchen, Rain Man had woken up and was sitting by his food bowl, crying for something to eat. Hannah picked him up and held him like a little baby. She dotted his nose with her finger and pontificated to him. "When you lose the ability to believe in even the possibility of love, you're the walking dead."

She put Rain Man down and opened a can of cat food for him. She went into the TV room and opened her laptop and started composing her letter to the editor of the *Baltimore Sun* newspaper. It read,

Dear Editor,

There is nothing wondrous about Colonel Rupert's Wildlife Wonderland Zoo. The Zoo's neglect of its animals, filthy conditions, and shoddy safety features make it an inadequate habitat for all the animals housed there. There are two African lions, Bobby and Babs, who are suffering the most. They live in an enclosure that is way too small for them. Both cats pace constantly, a clear sign of anxiety and frustration. Furthermore, even the most basic veterinary care is lacking. As of this writing, Bobby appears to have an untreated case of mange and Babs is limping.

These magnificent animals are being exploited for financial gain. They should be free, as God intended them. Instead, they are caged for human amusement and profit. I would encourage anyone reading this to boycott this inhumane business, a business built on

the misery of others.

Gandhi said, "The greatness of a nation and its moral progress can be judged by the way its animals are treated." If this is true, then our society is the moral equivalent of living in the Stone Age.

Hannah Cohen, Baltimore

Rain Man finished his food and wobbled his way into the room to join Hannah. He licked his chops and she read her letter back to him.

When she finished, she looked down at the cat, sighed and asked, "Well, what do you think, kid? There's a lot more I want to say, but they won't print anything that's terribly long. It has to be under two-hundred words or they'll reject it."

As she put a frozen pizza in the microwave, her phone alerted her that she had a text message from David.

Working on setting up Facebook page. What do u think of calling it Bobby and Babs: Born Free But Now Living in Misery? Also do u have any photos of the lions?

She replied, *I like, will send u photos later.*

Sounds good. Dress warm for the game, temps in the 40's. Looking forward to an evening with a lovely lady!

On a cold, raw early-spring day in Maryland, that last sentence in his text filled her with warmth. She closed her eyes, smiled, and daydreamed. She was almost happy that it would be so cold at the game and imagined David holding her against his chest. Only the microwave timer going off snapped her out of it. When she tasted the pizza, she looked at Rain Man and complained to him. "Now, this is the brand that's supposed to be as good as pizzeria pizza and it tastes like freaking cardboard. That was a waste of seven bucks." She threw the piece of pizza down. *I'd rather be having an egg salad sandwich on rye at Tiffany's.*

David sat at his computer and checked the pitching match-ups for the game. *Oh, geez. Gene* Grand Slam *Garrity's pitching for the O's.* Garrity had earned the nickname *Grand Slam* for his propensity for giving them up. David looked down at Brandi, his four-year-old brindle Pitbull and told her, "Well, we know this one's going in the loss column. But, tonight the game is secondary. I met a woman." Brandi looked up at him and cocked her ears. "Yeah. I'm serious. A woman. Imagine that. She's smart, nice, and pretty, too. The trifecta."

He checked his email. An advertisement from a website called *From Russia With Lust*, which promoted mail order brides. *How the hell did I get on that mailing list?* He shook his head. A reminder from Brandi's vet that she'd be due for shots next month. Updates from his fantasy baseball league. A message from the estate lawyer of a wealthy, Nigerian prince who had recently passed away and left David ten million dollars, payable pending the remittance of a one-time five-hundred-dollar *processing fee.* He laughed out loud as he deleted it. Finally, there was one from The Right Reverend Miles Higgins. *Aw, shit! What does he want? I'm on vacation.* The subject line read, *"Re – Your recent appearance on social media."* *This can't be good.* He rolled his eyes and read the message.

Dear David,

It was brought to my attention that you appeared in a video clip which was published on social media, one which has garnered considerable national attention. A so-called "viral video," if you will. Upon viewing the clip in question, I must tell you that I find it troubling. You appear wearing your clerical shirt and Roman collar. A young woman is pressing her body against yours. Her breasts are clearly contacting your chest. And your hands are pre-

cariously close to her backside. This is not the image that the
Church wishes to present to the world.

As a member of the clergy, you must observe certain rules of de-
corum – unwritten though they may be. I have no idea what the
nature of your relationship is with this young woman. I would,
however, remind you of the Church's position regarding what con-
stitutes a godly relationship between a man and a woman. I would
further remind you that it is the clergy's responsibility to set the
example.

I would encourage you to spend your energy finding ways to
enhance the image of the Church rather than finding new and in-
novative ways to embarrass it. We will discuss this matter in
greater detail once you return from your vacation.

As always, you are in my prayers.

Miles

"I need a cigarette," he told Brandi. He filled a plastic cup
with water to use as an ashtray and walked outside to the
rectory's front yard.

It was flurrying, something not unheard of in Maryland
in early April. He lit his smoke and shook his head in disgust. He talked to himself. "Why is he taking something so
innocent and turning it into something seedy? I don't understand that guy. What's his problem?"

He finished his cigarette and threw the butt into the cup,
then he went back inside and resolved not to let the bishop's
email ruin his day. "Gotta go do some shopping," he told
Brandi. "Don't worry, Daddy's going to bring you something home. How about some of those liver flavored treats
that you like so much? Hmm? Would you like that? Would
Daddy's little girl like that, huh?" Brandi wagged her tail
and barked excitedly. He picked the smallish Pitbull up and
hugged her and kissed her on the forehead.

Chapter Six: The Man on the Moon

Hannah looked at herself in the bedroom mirror. She had never given this much thought to dressing for a baseball game before. *I want to look sexy, but in a sweet way.* She let her hair out of its ponytail and applied her favorite perfume, Girl Next Door. She was dressed in jeans, a new white sneaker for her right foot and four pairs of heavy athletic socks for her left, and a black hoodie underneath a replica grey Orioles road jersey. A pink Orioles cap and two Orioles Eye Black stickers completed the look. She looked at her bar of soap-on-a-rope and wondered if she should take it with her. *Maybe I can try leaving it home just this once. No. Impossible.* She felt naked without it. Besides, he seemed to be okay with it. So far. *Oh, God, what if we get married? Will I be standing there at the altar with this damn bar of soap? It's all a tempest in a teapot at this point. You're getting way ahead of yourself.*

She looked at her phone and read some of the comments left about the diner video. It now had over two hundred thousand views. One comment, in particular, caught her attention.

To the young couple in this video — thank you for helping to rebuild my faith in humanity. My daughter, Amanda, was killed a few months ago, the victim of domestic violence. She was twenty years old. She never got to experience what real love is like. I'd like to believe that she was there in that diner that day. And that she danced right along with you and got a sense of what it would have been like to fall in love. Thank you! Love and Tears, Debbie —

Amanda's mom.

The doorbell rang. She looked at her watch. "Oh, gosh, he's so early," she told Rain Man. She gingerly maneuvered herself down the stairs on her butt. "Coming!" When she opened the door, she was met with the aroma of fresh red roses.

"For you," he told her as he walked inside. He was wearing an orange Orioles hooded sweatshirt, jeans, a pair of white Nikes, and an orange and black Orioles cap. Hannah couldn't help but notice how he filled out his jeans. She caught herself staring at his ass.

"They're lovely. Thank you." She took the flowers and placed them as the centerpiece on her yellow dinette table.

"Hey, I know I'm early, but I have a little gift for you before we head out."

"Oh, there was no need to do that. The flowers are more than enough."

"I wanted to." He presented her with a gift bag that had cute pictures of kittens on it.

She looked inside the bag. A digital voice recorder was the first item she pulled out.

"Every writer should have one," he told her. "That way, when you get an inspiration at two o'clock in the morning, you can just reach across your nightstand and record your idea instead of forgetting it."

"That's a wonderful and practical gift for a writer," she said. "Thank you."

"There's more. Keep going."

Next, she took out a book. *Writing Right: Tips for the First-Time Novelist.* "Now this is cool. Someone like me needs all the tips she can get."

"You're selling yourself short. You just need to take the leap and get started. And being a writer is a worthy vocation. Writers can change the world." He looked her in the eye. "And I think you're going to be a terrific writer."

He has more faith in me than I have in myself.

"Oh, and there's one more item in there," he said.

She pulled it out, covered her open mouth with her palm and let out a gasp.

"How . . . how did you know? How did you know this is my favorite?"

He shrugged, "I didn't for sure. It was an educated guess." He smiled.

An old, leather-bound, illustrated copy of Truman Capote's short story, "A Christmas Memory."

"It's one of the best short stories ever written," she told him.

"I wouldn't argue that point."

"It's so tender, sweet, and sincere," she said. She paused and put her head down and added, "Like you . . . like you."

"Go ahead and open it."

On the title page, it was signed by the author.

"Oh, my God! He signed this? Truman Capote signed this?" she asked.

He nodded. "Yes. The autograph's been authenticated. There's a COA for the signature issued by a very reputable company. It's in the bag, too, all the way at the bottom. They said he probably signed it sometime in the early nineteen sixties. I got it at a bookstore in the Inner Harbor that deals exclusively in rare books."

"But this must have cost a fortune. I don't know if I can accept something so valuable. I mean, the man's been dead for well over thirty years, so it's not like there are a whole lot of these items floating around anymore."

He shrugged his shoulders. "It was sitting on a shelf, literally collecting dust. It should be owned by someone who can appreciate it. Everything that's special should be loved and appreciated."

"Thank you." She hobbled over to him and hugged him.

They looked into each other's eyes. Each was looking into two pools of blue. The kind of blue that was like a cloudless spring sky. Peaceful, picturesque, pure. He held her up with his right hand and with his left, gently brushed a wisp of blonde hair out of her eyes.

Then, she lost her balance and began to teeter and started to fall backward.

"Woah!" she cried.

He caught her at the last possible moment, right before she hit the hardwood floor.

"I thought for sure I was going to fall! That was close."

"Like making the game-saving, shoestring catch in base-ball," he quipped. Then he added, "Seriously, I'd never let you fall. Never. But I might fall for —" He stopped abruptly, smiled and pulled her forward and she steadied herself.

"Fall for what?"

"You okay?" he asked.

She nodded "Ah-huh. But what is it that you might fall for?"

"I . . . I was just going to say that I kind of, sort of, feel myself falling for —"

Meow! Meow! Meow!

Rain Man was looking up at them, bobbing his head.

"He wants some attention," she said.

He reached down and picked the cat up and cuddled him. "Well, hello there, little man," he said as he gently scratched the cat under his chin.

Way to block momma, Rain Man.

Hannah hobbled over to the living room sofa and sat down.

He stroked Rain Man's head while the cat purred and told her, "It's not just big cats that I have a fondness for. I like the tiny tigers, too. I love animals in general. My dog is a shelter rescue. Brandi is her name, a four-year-old tiny little brindle Pitbull."

"You have a Pitbull?"

"I do. They're good dogs who are misunderstood. Brandi, for example, is scared of her own shadow. She loves everyone, including cats. You know, I pet sat a cat for a parishioner who was traveling to the UK for two weeks. Brandi thought the cat was her pup. Constantly grooming the little fellow, you know? It's important to see everyone as an individual. After all, that's how God sees us, right?"

He put Rain Man down and he immediately went over to his baby blue plush mouse stuffed with organic catnip and batted it.

Hannah smiled at him. "It's good that you see things that way. I wish everyone could."

He looked at his watch. "Well, I guess we should be heading to the game, huh?"

She picked up a blue and white public library tote bag which contained her purse and her old softball glove. "Yeah. I guess. I think I'm ready. I think I have everything I wanted to take with me."

"Oh, before we leave, I wanted to tell you that you look adorable tonight. Those Orioles Eye Black strips bring out your eyes. They're cute, too."

"Aw, very sweet of you to notice. That means a lot to me."

He opened the door for her and helped her in the passenger's seat.

"Such a gentleman. A *gentleman* and a *gentle man*," she noted with a smile. Then she lamented, "And *gentle men* are not as common as they should be."

The short drive from Federal Hill to Camden Yards took longer than normal. Rush hour combined with stadium traffic slowed them down.

He tuned in the pregame show on the radio.

"You know, I must say I was surprised—pleasantly—to

find that you are so knowledgeable about baseball."

"Yeah?"

"Yeah."

"Did you think that because I'm a woman that I wouldn't know much about sports?"

"I might have slipped into that mindset. You see, when I go to the games, I see a lot of *Woo Women*."

"*Woo Women*?"

"Yep. Those are the ones who sit there with their boy-friends or husbands and they have no idea as to what's go-ing on. They just sit there the entire time and go, *Woo!*"

She laughed. "Oh, gee, come to think of it, I've seen them, too. Occasionally one of them will say something like *come on! Hit a touchdown!* They spend more time fiddling with their freaking phones than they do watching the game. I'll bet you anything most of them are former sorority girls."

He laughed and nodded. "Probably."

"I like baseball because it's a game about fresh starts, new beginnings. Every spring, as the world is coming into bloom, the season starts and no matter how bad your team sucked the previous year, there's hope, you know? Hope that maybe by the time the Boys of Summer turn into the Men of Au-tumn, your team will be in the World Series. There's some-thing very poetic about that." She wondered if she sounded too philosophical, too much like George Will when he talked about his affinity for baseball.

He nodded. "That's exactly how I look at it. And I'll tell you something else, too — I think that if God plays a game, it would have to be baseball."

"Why?"

"Well, think about it. Of all the four major sports, baseball is the only game that's not timed. No quarters, no halves, no periods. You play nine innings — or more if it goes extra in-nings — and it doesn't matter how long it takes. In theory, a baseball game could go on for all eternity. And baseball is very forgiving. There's always a chance for redemption. Always. The guy who is the goat one day might hit a home run in the bottom of the ninth to win it the next. Like in the film version of *The Natural*. One man with one last chance to redeem himself, to take everything that was wrong and make it right. That's epic. Mythical. Even biblical. Plus, baseball brings people together instead of driving them apart. You sit in the upper deck on a sun-drenched summer afternoon, smell the beer and the hot dogs, and people from different backgrounds all cheer for the same thing. They might not agree on anything else, but they can all agree that baseball is a great game."

"So if God plays baseball, what team would He play for?" she asked.

"The Angels or the Padres . . . *ba-dum-ching*."

She rolled her eyes. "Awful. Just awful. That was worse than the one you told about the Tanning Olympics."

"Hey, you provided such a great setup. I couldn't waste it."

She looked at him, licked her lips, and brushed her hair with her hand. "Tell me something about yourself that no one else knows?"

He turned the radio down. "Something that no one else knows?"

After about ten seconds he told her, "I'm kind of drawing a blank here."

There was a long pause as she looked at him expectantly.

"Oh! Got one. You ready for this?"

"Yeah,"

"Okay. Well, I own land on the moon."

She burst into laughter. "On the *moon*?"

"Yep. I purchased it for fifty bucks from the International Lunar Land Registry. I am the proud owner of *Tract Eight-*

een, Parcel 1021 on Mare Moscoviense. I was wanting to get into the Sea of Tranquility area, but I wasn't about to pay the
broker's asking price. The Sea of Tranquility—I guess that's
the lunar equivalent of The Hamptons. So I know it's all
about *location, location, location,* but, still, you've got to stick
to your budget."

Still laughing she asked, "What possessed you to buy
land on the freaking moon?"

He shrugged his shoulders. "A conversation piece. You're
at a boring cocktail party and some self-important rich guy
is bragging about how he just bought this gorgeous piece of
property in Rehoboth. Then I could come back with *oh yeah,
fella? Well, I own land on the moon. So top that!* Haven't had a
chance to use it yet, but it's comforting to know that I have it
up my sleeve if I ever need it."

She stopped laughing long enough to tell him, "If every
minister was as colorful and interesting as you, the churches
would be full on Sunday mornings." She thought for a
moment and then she added, "Your sense of humor is so
corny sometimes. But it's harmless, utterly harmless. It's not
mean-spirited. It's not designed to hurt anyone."

"Well, you couldn't very well laugh if you were hurting
someone."

She noted that he said it so matter-of-factly. As if it was a
total no-brainer, the most obvious thing in the world. She
nodded and took in the measure of the man in that one simple sentence. Only an exceptional person would say something like that, she decided.

"Okay, now it's your turn," he said. "Tell me one of your
secrets."

*Not about to tell him my big secret, not yet anyway. We'll start
with something that's not such a bombshell.*

"Well, you know that song, *I Just Called to Say I Love You?*
The Stevie Wonder song."

"Sure, I know it. Great song. By the way, did you hear

that Stevie is recording a new, updated version of that song?"

She got an incredulous look on her face. "He is? I didn't hear about that."

"Yeah, it's called *I Just Texted to Say I Love You.*"

"Can you please be serious for just a minute? Come on! I'm trying to share something personal with you here. This is important."

"I'm sorry. I promise—no more jokes."

She looked down. "I hope you don't think I'm weird after you hear this."

"Hey, I own land on the moon and was traded for beer. I've got the market cornered on weirdness." He took his right hand off the steering wheel, gently patted her left hand, and briefly took his eyes off the road just long enough to warmly smile at her.

She cracked a smile despite herself. "Okay. Well, every time I hear that song, I start bawling. And I mean really bawling. We're not talking a gentle trickle of tears. We're talking a deluge."

"It's a pretty song. A lot of people are moved to tears by beautiful songs. I'm not too proud to admit that *Come Sail Away* always gets to me."

"But that's not why I cry when I hear it. They're not tears of joy. They really are tears of sadness."

"So why does a happy song make you sad?

"Because no one has ever, in my entire life, called me just to tell me that they love me."

She looked over at him and her lower lip began to quiver a tad. Tears made tracks down her cheeks like a car driving on an unplowed, snow-covered road.

She was waiting for his reaction. *If he can't handle this, there's no way he can handle my real baggage.*

He reached over and held her hand. She closed her eyes and felt the warmth of his hand. And his warmth filled her with warmth. The same kind of warmth that one gets from lowering oneself into a hot bath on a cold winter's day. She felt safe and hopeful.

They parked on the stadium lot and could smell the barbeque chicken, cotton candy, and hotdogs of street vendors.

Hannah tentatively pulled out a cigarette from her purse. "I kind of smoke. Do you mind if I have one before we go in?"

"Good idea. I'll burn one, too." He tapped out a Camel from its pack.

"You smoke, too?" she asked.

"Unfortunately."

"When we were at Tiffany's, I thought I could smell smoke on you, but I wasn't sure," she said.

"Same here. I wasn't sure whether I was smelling my own smoke or yours."

He lit her Virginia Slims for her. She noticed that the onyx ring he'd worn at the zoo had given way to an even gaudier one. This one was gold, encrusted with diamonds, and showed a royal flush. It was a pinky ring, too. She stared at it.

"That's some serious bling you have there, fella," she said as she pointed to the ring.

He held his hand in front of his face to admire it. He looked at her and smiled. "Like it?"

She smiled back and teased him. "You sure you don't work for a guy named Pauly?"

"I always wear it to the games. It brings good luck. A royal flush is the luckiest hand you can get in poker."

"You believe in luck?"

"Sure I do. Ballplayers are very superstitious. Once, I ate a corned beef sandwich for lunch on a day I pitched. I didn't make it out of the first inning. Gave up eight runs and three homers in only two-thirds of an inning. I never ate corned beef again, even to this day."

"So I guess you're going to tell me that after you gave up corned beef, you always pitched great."

He laughed and shook his head. "No. I wouldn't say that. There was one benefit though."

"And what was that?"

"My indigestion cleared up."

She shook her head in mock disgust. "You're always setting up your next punchline, aren't you?"

He turned serious. He put his head down, his hands in his pockets, and kicked some pebbles at his feet. "Hey, while we're just standing here, I, ah, I actually kind of wanted to ask you something." She could detect the nervousness in his voice.

He took a deep breath, cleared his throat and began. "Well, see, I'm on vacation—as you know—and the Diocese has this house down in Ocean City. It's a nice house and they use it for retreats, but they also allow the clergy to stay there. It's large. Very large. And it's right on the beach. I mean, literally, the ocean is in the backyard. So I was wondering, since you're off work for a while, maybe you'd like to go down with me. I have the place for a whole week."

"Go down with you?"

He looked up at her with big eyes. "Yes. I promise it would be completely proper. Needless to say, you'd have your own room and all. I don't want you to think that I'm a cad."

She smiled. "A *cad*, huh?"

"Yeah, you know, a jerk, a rogue. A scoundrel."

She took a deep drag on her cigarette and began speaking with the smoke still in her lungs. "David, I was an *English* major. I know what the word *cad* means. It just isn't a word you hear used much anymore. It's a word that the male lead would have used in some old movie. You know, it'd be something like *darling, please don't think I'm a cad just because I bet the boys down at the country club that I could win a date with you.*"

"All right. Very funny. But let's move beyond my use of antiquated vocabulary. Would you like to go?"

"I would actually love to, but what about Rain Man? I don't have anyone who would be able to take care of him."

"Bring him."

"Really?"

"Sure. I'm bringing Brandi. And Ocean City is great this time of year. The summer crowds aren't there yet, but the boardwalk and everything is open. C'mon. What do you say?"

She nodded. "I'd like that."

"Yeah?"

"Yeah. Definitely."

She could see a look of relief come over his face as he spoke. "Cool. So how about if I pick you guys up tomorrow afternoon?"

"Great. Could we stop by the zoo first, though, to see Bobby and Babs?"

"Sure. Maybe we can get some video of them and send it to the Finally Free Foundation."

They headed for the stadium's Eutaw Street entrance. Hannah propelled herself along on her crutches and David carried her tote bag and a brown, paper shopping bag that he brought along that contained some peanuts, radio headphones, boxed juice, and an extra jacket.

As they approached the stadium entrance, a street hustler was hawking his wares. He sported dreadlocks, gold teeth and peddled fake Rolexes and Muslim oils. When he saw David's flashy ring, he called out, "I can see you have excellent taste, playa. Why don't you come over here and let me set you up with one of my fine Rollies? I have a special sale price for G's like yourself—only one c note. We could have you lookin' classier than Kanye."

They walked past the man without acknowledging his sales pitch. David turned to Hannah and got a quizzical look on his face. "Did he just call me a *player* and a *G?*" They laughed as they presented their tickets and entered through the turnstiles.

Their seats were in the second row, near the Yankees' dugout on the third base side. They were outstanding seats. She was impressed, as she looked around and took in the scents—beer, hotdogs, crab cakes, cotton candy, and peanuts. All mixed together to create that distinct aroma unique to ballparks.

Seated directly in front of them were two well-dressed older men. One of them wore a bad toupee and too much of what Hannah recognized as Aramis cologne. The other was chomping on an unlit cigar. They alternated between watching the game and thumbing through copies of *The Daily Racing Form*. As they perused the magazine, they discussed strategy for betting the trifecta in the next day's first race at Laurel Park. The one with the cigar nudged the other and pointed to a page. "Sentimental Journey, Yars' Revenge, and Hopeless Romantic. Win. Place. Show. I'm putting a hundred on it. But for Christ's sake, don't tell Helen. She doesn't know that I started going back to the track." David smirked, and Hannah rolled her eyes and shook her head.

In the next section over, there was an elderly couple who held up a homemade sign for the television cameras which read, *Today is our 50th anniversary and all we want is an Orioles win!* Hannah looked at them, smiled, and hoped that one day she'd be celebrating a 50th anniversary.

She dug into her tote bag and pulled out her glove from her days of playing college softball.

Slamming her right fist into the mitt's pocket, she told

him, "I'm ready to grab a foul ball. I've never gotten one before, but in these seats, I just might."

"I've gotten a few fouls sitting here over the years," he
said.

"You sit here all the time?"

"Yeah. These are my season ticket seats. I have the
twenty-game mini-plan. I like these seats not only for the
great view but because you don't have to worry about putting up with the drunks. People who put out money for field
box seats are here to actually watch the game, not drink and
party."

"Does someone normally come with you?"

"No."

"So you come to all these games alone?'

"Yeah."

"So why did you buy two season tickets?"

He looked at her and then looked down. She could tell he
was embarrassed. "Because, I hope that someday, maybe
someday, I'll have someone who I can take to the games
with me."

They were in a stadium with thirty thousand other people, but at that moment, to her, it was just the two of them.
She put her hand on top of his and gently squeezed it.

She started to tilt her head to the right to place it on his
shoulder. Then a group of teenage girls came bounding
down the concrete steps, squealing and holding cell phones.

One, no older than thirteen, had braces and was wearing
a sweatshirt depicting a kitten riding a unicorn. "It's Reverend Romance!" the girl gushed. "Can we take a selfie with
you? You're up to something like two-hundred-fifty-
thousand views now. WJZ even showed the footage on its
Rise N' Shine morning show today." Before they could answer, the little girl was posing and snapping the photo.

She pointed to David and asked Hannah, "He your steady

boo?"

"My boo?" Hannah knew what the word meant, but had been taken aback by the girl's casual nosiness.

"Yeah, you know—your *man*," the little girl barked with attitude. Before Hannah had a chance to answer she pressed further, nonchalantly asking, "Are you guys married or are you just shacking up? My dad says shacking is the way to go because you get all the benefits without any of the pains in the ass. Says he wishes he had just shacked up with my mom—hey, can I get a smoke?"

David intervened. "Little girl, that type of language is not very becoming of a young lady and you are *way* too young to be talking about people shacking up. And you most certainly are not going to get a cigarette from either of us. Now, go! Go home!"

The girl rolled her eyes and gave him the *stop hand.* "Oh, *whatever!*" She then walked over to Hannah and wagged her little finger in her face, bobbed her head from side to side, and issued a warning, "Better watch that man of yours! I stole Timmy Bateman from Sarah Thompson at the Sadie Hawkins dance. Give me another five years or so to catch up to you and I'll have your man, too, bitch! Um hmm!"

Hannah sat with her mouth open in shock, unable to formulate a response. The little girl stormed off giggling, while the other girls in her entourage looked back at Hannah and laughed, with one of them telling her, "Guess she told *you,* girl!"

Hannah forced an uneasy smile. "Precocious little monster, isn't she?"

David shook his head and said, "She looked like she was barely a teenager and she's talking about stealing men and shacking up. Thirteen going on thirty. Call me old-fashioned, but kids are growing up way too fast nowadays."

"I know. Seriously."

He continued to sermonize. "And you know, when they're barely a teenager and talking like that already, what are they going to turn into in five or ten years? Probably a stripper or something, that's what."

His statement reminded her of what Nicki had told her. And it caused her mind to become overloaded like a computer with too many windows open. *Once he finds out, he'll never want me. I've got to quit, not just for him, but for me, too. But then what will I do for money? God, the money is so good. But I hate it, I hate how it makes me feel about myself. I have to get out of it. I have to.*

She stopped paying attention to the game and zoned out, preoccupied with the complexity of her situation.

"You hungry?" he asked.

"Um, no. I'm okay."

"You sure?"

"Um hmm. Maybe later, though."

"Hey, here's an idea—on the way home, why don't we stop at Tiffany's? They're open twenty-four seven, so it won't matter what time the game ends. We can get some egg salad."

The suggestion lifted her spirits a little. "Yeah. That'll work. Tiffany's sounds good,"

Between the top and bottom of the seventh inning, the PA system blared the Orioles traditional seventh-inning stretch song, *Thank God I'm A Country Boy*. They stood with the rest of the crowd. As Hannah leaned on her crutches and daintily clapped in rhythm to the music, David tentatively put his left arm around her. She briefly looked over at him, smiled, rested her head on his shoulder, and kept clapping."

By the top of the eighth inning, the cold was biting hard.

"Are you warm enough?" he asked.

"Well, it is getting really chilly. And I forgot to bring my Orioles quilted jacket."

He reached into the brown shopping bag and pulled out a

coat.

"Here you go. You can slip this on if you'd like." It was a Bel Air Bay Cats warm-up jacket, royal blue with black sleeves. The word *Bay Cats* was embroidered on the front in white script lettering. *O'Malley* was embroidered on the back in script.

"This was part of my official uniform issue."

"Thanks." She gingerly stood up and slipped it on. Far too big, it hung down past her waist, longer than some mini-skirts, and her hands disappeared into sleeves designed for someone with very long arms. Only the very bottom portion of her soap-on-a-rope was still visible.

"How do I look?" she asked, as she flailed the excess sleeves around.

"Cute."

"Really?"

"Really."

He thought for a moment and got a devilish look on his face. "Yep. Now all you need is a big wad of chewin' tabackey in your mouth and you'd look like a real ballplayer," he said, as he gently smacked the bill of her cap down so that it completely covered her eyes.

With the cap still pushed down, she asked, "Wouldn't you be embarrassed to be seen hanging out with a woman who spits tobacco juice?"

"Only if you could spit it farther than me, kiddo."

She pushed the visor of the cap upwards, just enough so that she could see, and then looked up at the sky.

"Oh, David! Look at it. Look at that big, orange moon tonight."

It was as if the huge orange disk was emitting a gentle warmth that seemed to take a little bit of the chill off that night.

He looked up. "It looks so close. Like you could reach out

and touch it."

She nodded in awe, then smiled and asked, "Can you see your parcel of land?"

"Nah. It's on the dark side of the moon. The low rent district."

"Imagine what this moon looks like in Africa, in the bush of Africa. Away from all the city lights. Imagine Bobby and Babs lying under an Acacia Tree and gazing up at this moon, knowing that they're free, free to go anywhere," she said.

"Free to go anywhere that their dreams take them," he added.

"Yes. Exactly. Isn't that beautiful?"

"Sure it is. That sentiment is beautiful, this moon's beautiful." He paused and then looked at her and continued, "But there's something about tonight that's even more beautiful."

"And what's that?" she asked expectantly. *Okay, pal, there's only one right answer here and it's not the lush, green grass of the Camden Yards outfield.*

"You, Hannah Cohen." *Aw, good boy. Winner winner chicken dinner.*

She waited. But he just smiled at her.

Finally, she broke the silence. "You're shy, aren't you? I mean, on the surface, you're outgoing but when it comes to women, you're really shy."

"I suppose I am. See, I do want to kiss you." He paused and then broke into his own imitation of a 1940s male romantic lead, "But I don't want you to think that I'm a cad, darling."

"Well, since you want to talk old Hollywood, this is the part of the picture where the camera would focus in on the moon, then on us. And we would kiss. A long, passionate but supremely tender kiss. And the camera would pan out to show us still kissing as that big, beautiful moon shone down on us. Then the music, some lavish orchestra, would well up and play some sweet theme song. And the people in the theater would be crying because it was so beautiful and lovely. People would go home feeling better about the world. That's what the script calls for." She thought for a moment and added, "So in other words, I'll only think you're a cad if you don't kiss me, darling."

"So you want me to kiss you in front of all these people. There must be at least thirty thousand people here tonight."

Remembering what he had told her in the diner, she nodded. "Then let those thirty thousand people know that the two of us are free enough that we don't care what they think."

He nodded approvingly. "Very good. I'm impressed."

He gently ran the back of his hand along her cheek. She had never been touched with such gentleness. An audible sigh escaped her lips and she closed her eyes. Goosebumps erupted on her forearms. She could feel herself becoming aroused. For Hannah, horniness was a natural byproduct of romance.

"Well, in the interest of preserving the integrity of the script . . ." He drew her into him and placed his large hand under her chin and gently tilted her head up. He went in for the kiss and his forehead ran into the visor of her ball cap, which she always wore lower than most people. With mock exasperation, he threw up his hands and said, "Now, you see, that's the trouble with tomboys. When you want to kiss one, you end up running into the bill of her ball cap, and it blocks you, like a nun blocking a kiss at a Catholic junior high dance." He took the cap off of her head and turned it around and placed it on her head backward. "There. That was an easy enough problem to solve. And it looks even sexier on backward anyway." Then he again drew her into him and kissed her.

After only a couple of seconds, she could feel him start to pull away. But she was having none of that. As she felt him start to retreat, she took her hands, invisible because of the long sleeves of the jacket, pulled him deeper into her, and opened her mouth. She felt him loosen up and his mouth opened as well. Using her tongue like a paintbrush, she frantically and haphazardly attempted to coat the inside of his mouth with her saliva.

It turned into something of a spectacle. The stadium *Kiss Cam* found them and broadcast their first kiss on the Camden Yards Jumbotron. The local cable television network made it part of their live telecast, all but guaranteeing that it would make the evening's *Sports Center* highlight reel. When they finally unlocked lips, they leaned their heads forward so that their foreheads were touching. The fans around them were cheering, even the Yankee fans, but they themselves were oblivious. It was just the two of them and the moon. That big, marvelous moon. For the longest time, they looked into each other's eyes.

Finally, she broke the silence and said, "That was nice. Really nice. My legs even feel a little weak. You hit a home run." She giggled.

He said nothing, just looked into her eyes and smiled.

She cleared her throat and told him, "I do believe this is the part where you're supposed to agree with me and tell me how wonderful it was for you as well."

He laughed. "Sorry. I was just thinking."

"About what?"

"About that moon up there."

She got an agitated look on her face. "About the moon? She pointed upwards. "That heavenly body is a quarter of a million miles away." She then pointed to herself. "But *I'm* right in front of you. So why, pray tell, are you thinking about the moon?"

He again laughed. "Whoa. Hold on. Just give me a chance to explain."

"Okay. But this better be good," she said as she gave him the evil eye.

He took a deep breath and began. "I was thinking about the moon and how it's so familiar but still so mysterious. I mean, consider it. We can all see it, almost every night, in fact. But only twelve men, out of the tens of billions of humans who have ever lived, have been there, have walked on it. The Men of the Moon — they're the only ones who understand. They're the only ones who can truly have an intimate connection. They're the only ones who've really taken in its desolate majesty. For the rest of us, it's still an enigma. We can never know what it's *really* like. For me, at least, that's kind of what romance has always been like. Familiar but mysterious. I perform weddings and counsel couples all the time, but I've never really understood what it was all about. But tonight . . . well, tonight, I feel like Neil Armstrong. Like the man on the moon."

She smiled at him and tenderly caressed his cheek with her hand. "It comforts me to hear you say that."

"Oh yeah? How so?"

An ornery grin crossed her face. "Now I know, despite all of your idiosyncrasies — which are *many* — that at least you're not some nutty conspiracy theorist who doesn't believe that they put a man on the moon."

He laughed heartily and shook his index finger at her. "That may be true, but there are some conspiracy theories which I wholeheartedly embrace. For example, I firmly believe that both Elvis and Andy Kaufman faked their own deaths. In fact, I'll take it one step further and say that Andy Kaufman and Elvis were the same person. I mean, think about it — they kind of resembled one another and they were never seen together. And who was the best Elvis impersonator of all-time? Andy Kaufman, that's who. And I'll bet you anything Elvis was the best Andy Kaufman impersonator."

He winked at her and grinned.

With mock exasperation, she told him, "Oh, you're incorrigible. Really, you are." Then she kissed him again.

The Yankees beat the Orioles that night. Bam-Bam Bradford got ahold of a fastball that was hung out over the middle of the plate in the top of the ninth and hit a grand slam home run off Orioles' relief pitcher, Tony Clifton, to lift the Bronx Bombers to a 6-5 win. Clifton should have thrown him a changeup or slider because Bradford was sitting on the fastball. Bigtime.

When they left the stadium, it was getting colder still. Snow showers passed through the area.

She looked up at the snow that was illuminated by the street lights. "So weird. We just watched a baseball game in football weather."

"That's Maryland for you. This time of the year, you can experience all fours seasons in a single day."

"Even with the cold and snow, it was a lovely evening. But it would have been great if the Orioles could have won for us," she lamented.

"Well, tonight I think we just got caught between the moon and the New York Yankees. I know it's crazy, but it's true."

They stopped, and she looked up at him. She'd gotten his play on words. "And what's the best that you can do when that happens?" she asked. He cupped her cheek with his hand, put his arm around her waist and pulled her into him. He was about to speak when a car blared its horn. They had stopped right in the middle of Eutaw Street without even thinking about it.

"Hey, buddy! The Charm City Motel's right across the street. Get a room!" a cab driver yelled out his window.

"Sorry about that, sir," David apologized and waved at the driver. Then he smiled at her and they resumed their trek to the parking lot.

He opened the Town Car's door for her and before she got in, they paused and looked again at that moon. They looked at it through the fog of their exhaled breaths and the wet snow. He again pulled her close. She closed her eyes, took in the scent of his cologne, and nuzzled against his chest. And she wondered. She wondered—if there had been a man on the moon that night, whether he could have seen lights pulsing from the Earth, from downtown Baltimore. Two hearts coming together and radiating a kaleidoscope of warm colors, with those lights being shot toward the heaven like fireworks. She at least entertained the notion that such a phenomenon could be so powerful that it might actually be visible, even from the depths of outer space. And that if the man on the moon or God Himself or any other Intelligence that might have been out there had witnessed it, they might have known that in a world where people locked up lions in tiny cages that, this, too, was humanity.

As they drove off into the night, they listened to the post-game fan call-in show on the radio, with all its recriminations about who was at fault for giving up the grand slam homer to Bam-Bam. The pitcher for throwing the pitch? The catcher for calling the pitch? The manager for not putting a better pitcher and catcher in the game? Or God Himself for not damning the Yankees? Then, David tuned in an oldies station that happened to be playing R.E.M.'s *Man on the Moon*. They both laughed and sang along as the Lincoln cruised up the Jones Falls Expressway, towards Loch Raven Boulevard, en route to a late-night rendezvous with egg salad sandwiches at Tiffany's.

CHAPTER SEVEN: OF DOGS AND DOGMA

David got up early on Tuesday morning. He put on a pair of sweatpants and a hoodie and went outside. There was a thin coating of wet snow on the lawn. He walked to the mailbox to retrieve his copy of *The Baltimore Sun*. With newspapers, he still preferred a hard copy to digital. He briskly walked inside, sat at the kitchen table and turned to the sports section. On the front page, there was a large photo of him and Hannah kissing at the game, with the headline, *Who's Winning? Who Cares?!*

As he started to read the accompanying caption, his cell phone rang—the bishop. He wanted to ignore the call, but he knew that if he did, it would hang over his head for the rest of the day. Definitely, it would be better to take the call now and get it over with, he reasoned.

The bishop had seen the sports page as well and wasn't happy. He went on and on about how such undignified public displays of affection made a mockery of the church. David looked down at Brandi, rolled his eyes and shook his head. He held the phone away from his ear and sighed. Finally, he put the phone back up to his ear and spoke. "I'm sorry you feel that way, sir. I don't think I did anything wrong. Frankly, I think maybe what we need are more *public displays of affection* to counter all the public displays of aggression that are becoming common in our society." With that, he abruptly turned the phone off and dropped it on the kitchen table. He told Brandi, "What a prick." He thought a moment and added, "But we're not going to let him bring us down, girl." He clapped his hands and, in an exaggerated Baltimore accent, told the little Pitbull, "We're going to the ocean, hon!" Brandi barked excitedly and followed him into the den. The two sat on a black leather sofa and watched the DVR recording of the Capitals-Islanders game from the previous night.

After twenty minutes, the doorbell rang. When he opened the front door, he was greeted by Natalie Anderson, the head of St. Anne's Altar Guild. Natalie was in her forties, with bleached blonde hair, bleached white teeth, and an artificial tan that was darker than David's. Her husband was a wealthy real estate developer, and David suspected that she'd had several cosmetic procedures, including some bad lip implants.

Muriel loved to gossip. David had noticed that she always seemed to know everyone's business. Whether they were getting divorced, going bankrupt, or dying, she always seemed to be the first to know.

He forced a smile. "Hello, Muriel. What can I do for you?"

"Just need you to unlock the church for me. I'm going to polish the silver."

"Oh, it's unlocked."

She flashed a leery look. "It is? I thought the bishop ordered you to start locking it."

He nodded. "You're very well-informed." He paused and continued, "He did instruct me to lock it, but I decided that was inconsistent with this Church's mission."

There was an awkward paused. Finally, she replied, "Oh . . . I see."

"Anyway, it's open."

Muriel nodded and turned to walk away, but then she turned around and walked back up to the door.

"Oh, Father O'Malley," she called out.

"Yes."

"I saw you on TV last night. Larry was watching the ball-game and he calls me into his den and he says to me—he says—*there's Father O'Malley, on live TV playing tonsil hockey with the girl from the YouTube clip.* So what's this young lady's name?

"Hannah."

Muriel nodded approvingly. "Hannah. Nice name. Very biblical. Well, at least very Old Testament. She's quite pretty, too."

He smiled. "I agree. She is pretty. And nice. Very nice."

She wagged her finger at him. "You know, a lot of us were starting to wonder if you even liked women. Not that there would necessarily be anything wrong if you didn't, mind you. Nowadays, that kind of thing is perfectly acceptable, you know."

He smiled. "Yeah, well, I do. I do like women."

Muriel laughed. "I guess you're one of those metrosexuals. Now, those are men who act gay even though they aren't." He noted that she said it with pride, as if she was imparting some little-known morsel of knowledge.

He nodded and started to close the door. "I know what a metrosexual is. Thank you though."

"Ah, any chance we'll be seeing Hannah in church?"

He shook his head. "I doubt it." He again began to close the door.

"Is she not Anglican?"

"No, she's not Anglican."

"What denomination is she?"

"She's not Christian. She's Jewish."

He could see her face register shock and then an uneasy smile settled in. She shrugged her shoulders and said, "Well, I guess that's better than being Muslim." She laughed. Then she turned serious and added, "And maybe she'll get saved. I'll pray for her."

The comment made him angry. His heart raced. He was about to make a comment that he knew had the potential to start something. "What does she need to be saved from?" he asked. He made no effort to hide his agitation.

There was silence for a couple of seconds. Finally, Muriel said, "I think I'll head over to the Church. I'm sorry to have bothered you. I just thought it was locked. I didn't realize that you had disregarded the bishop's order."

"It's quite all right."

"Okay then. Oh, and I know you're going away for a couple of weeks. Have a *lovely* vacation."

He could detect the phoniness in her voice. "I'll try."

Finally, she was gone. He let out a deep breath and closed the door. As he walked back into the living room, he picked his cellphone up off the kitchen table and shoved it into the pocket of his sweatpants. He sat back down on the sofa with Brandi.

Petting the dog's head, he told her, "That's why I sometimes prefer the company of animals to the company of people. You guys never ask any nosy questions."

The TV was still playing, and he settled in to try to concentrate on the hockey game. But he couldn't get his encounter with Muriel off his mind. He continued to talk to Brandi. "I think she was truly disappointed that I'm straight. But she loved the fact that Hannah's Jewish. That's how some people are, girl. They're not happy unless, in their mind at least, they have something to be indignant about." He imagined Muriel sitting around at the next Church spaghetti dinner, whispering to other parishioners, "*That girl that he's running around with . . . well, she's Jewish. Oh yes. Jewish. He told me that himself!*"

He turned down the volume on the TV and pulled out his phone. He scrolled through his music. "Let's find something to get me out of this mood."

Eventually, he decided on one of his favorites, *More Than Words*, by Extreme, and turned up the volume. He threw his head back and closed his eyes. As the lyrics penetrated his soul, all he could think was that it was the perfect song for the moment. *It's action that gives meaning to words.* And he thought it was just as true in matters of the spirit as it was in matters of the heart.

He again talked to his dog. "No one *gets saved.* You save yourself by the way you choose to live. Whatever faith someone has is shown through action, not words. I don't think words impress God at all unless they're backed up by deeds."

He rubbed Brandi's head and gave her a big smile. She looked up at him with adoring eyes. "You dogs don't care what religion a person is so long as they feed you, walk you and love you—right?" She cocked her ears.

"I think that's what I love most about you guys—that there's no dogma in dogs." He leaned down and kissed her on her forehead.

Nicki texted Hannah to tell her that she and David had made *The Sun* sports page and that the clip of them kissing was being aired on ESPN and various social media plat-forms. Hannah texted back, explaining that she was going to the beach that afternoon and wouldn't be around for a week. Within an hour, Hannah and Nicki were standing on Han-nah's front porch smoking and talking about Hannah's im-promptu vacation.

Nicki took a long drag, then talked through her exhaled smoke, telling Hannah, "Going away together—that's a huge step."

"I know. But I'm ready. Oh! Last night was so wonderful.

It was one of those nights you never forget. I saved my ticket stub because thirty, forty years from now, I'll be able to tell the grandkids about that night. It was like something out of one of those old movies that you're so cynical about. And he's definitely not gay. But I do think he's metro. I mean, he always smells good, he's very neat and has a good fashion sense. Nice teeth. Hair never out of place. He goes to a tanning salon. Likes the soaps. Likes cats. I do wish he would stop wearing those garish rings, though. Last night, he wore this huge, hideous gold ring. It looked like something Sammy Davis Jr. would have worn." She rolled her eyes but then added, "But, if that's his biggest flaw, I'll definitely give him a pass on it. Besides, my soap-on-a-rope is my own gaudy piece of jewelry, I suppose." She glanced down at the bar of soap.

Nicki ignored the issue with the jewelry and seized on the real story — Hannah's alleged snaring of a metrosexual. "Get out of here! A metro? This is huge. Huge."

"What? Because he's metro?"

"*Yes!* Why are you so blasé about this? Don't you know what that means? I'm . . . I'm not sure you've grasped the significance of this, the implications, the ramifications. For a woman, finding an available metro is like . . . it's like . . . it's like finding the freaking Holy Grail, Atlantis, and Bigfoot all in the same day. Seriously, if you've got yourself a metro, that's rarer than a damn panda being born in captivity. I'd sell my soul to get myself one. The possibilities are endless. Endless! I mean, if you run out of exfoliator, you can *borrow his*. And you've got a man who won't be all whiny during shopping excursions. In fact, you'll be all like *honey, we've been in the mall all day – can't we go home?* And he'll be all like *girl, we haven't even been to Sephora yet, let alone Pottery Barn and Bed, Bath and Beyond.* He'll *knock* boots with you and then help you *pick out* boots. He'll make love *to* you, then make quiche *for* you. I mean, you've got the perfect guy. It'll be all

80

sex, shopping, pedicures, and movies based on Nicholas Sparks novels. What more could you want?"

They both threw their heads back and laughed.

"I never thought of it that way. I guess that could have its advantages," Hannah confessed.

Nicki flashed a sly smile and steered the conversation back to her favorite topic. "And speaking of sex . . . you guys are definitely going to have to do it soon, right?"

Hannah tapped the ash off her smoke with her index finger. "I want to. I feel very horny. I think I'll give him a lap dance when my ankle heals. I mean, I'm good at it, but when I do it at Polecats, it doesn't turn me on at all. It makes me feel dirty, shameful. But this would be different. Love is a game changer. I might have an orgasm just from grinding on him." They both giggled like school girls before Hannah continued, "But I'm not sure how he feels about that. I mean, he's an ordained minister. I think they tend to think that people should wait until marriage."

Nicki held her cigarette between her forefinger and middle finger and pointed it at Hannah for emphasis. "And that's one of the many reasons I'm not religious. Too many bullshit rules. If two people care about one another, why should it be wrong for them to have sex?"

Hannah shrugged her shoulders. "I didn't say it was."

Nicki continued, "If there is a God, that's one of the many questions I'd have for Him."

"I think He'd say that He's for love. I think He loves to see people fall in love, and that there's a celebration in Heaven every time it happens. It's like His own personal Hallmark Channel movie. He sits there with His box of tissues and bag of popcorn, and when they fall in love, He cries and walks away feeling hopeful about His world and tells the Four Horseman to hold their horses."

"Well, I don't know about any of that stuff, but I do know

that if you want to set the mood for sex, the best thing to do is to feed him."

"Feed him?"

"Yeah. Cook for him. A nice, big meal."

"Cooking for him will make him more likely to have sex with me?" Hannah thought Nicki was talking nonsense, trying to sound like she knew more about the inner workings of the male mind than she really did. Nonetheless, she was curious to hear the explanation.

"Yup. Food is like an aphrodisiac for men. After a big, satisfying meal, any inhibitions he has about the *sinfulness* of premarital sex will go right out the window. All men, even metros and ministers, are basically food whores. Cook him a nice pot roast—the kind with the little potatoes and carrots around it—and he'll fuck you all night long, girl. Guaranteed. Hell, throw in an apple pie for dessert and he'll probably even go down on you if you want."

"Oh, that's ridiculous! That almost sounds like a form of bribery. And I have enough confidence in my powers as a woman that I know I certainly don't have to bribe anyone into having sex with me. Besides, love doesn't need to use coercion. We'll make love when we're both ready."

"So you think that you're in love with this guy, huh?"

"Uh-huh." Hannah nodded emphatically and smiled a huge smile.

Nicki looked her up and down carefully. "I swear, I can see that you have a glow about you. I mean that literally, too. Your skin is always beautiful but, today it looks radiant."

"It's funny you should say that because the waitress at Tiffany's told me the same thing last night. It's amazing—the connection between body and mind."

"And you think he's falling in love with you, too?"

"I do. I really do. He almost said it last night. But then a dumb old cab driver beeped his horn at us just because we were standing in the middle of Eutaw Street."

"If all this is true, you're going to force him to make a choice. Because when he finds out about your life, there will be pressure on him to dump you. You know that, right?"

"He'll choose love. I know he will."

Nicki shook her head. "Life isn't some old Audrey Hepburn movie, honey. People *don't* always choose love in real life. In real life, people are practical, pragmatic. They take the path of least resistance. They aren't always brave. They don't always choose an abstract ideal over tangible things. Things like a job and their standing in the community. You know?"

Hannah mashed her cigarette in the ashtray and crossed her arms. "You're not going to do this to me. You're not going to bring me down today with your attitude. I'm going to the beach with a wonderful man, and we are going to have a perfectly lovely time. And, yes, we are going to make *mad, passionate* love. Maybe even on the beach. At sunset, no less. And you, Nicole Malone, are envious. Because deep down, you wish this was all happening to you."

"Oh. Pa-lease. You're setting yourself up for a big fall, dear. Go. Go ahead and play house for a week and when you get back with a broken heart, bawling your eyes out, I'll have to pick up the pieces. Yet again. Like I said before — you'll never learn." Nicki shook her head in disgust.

"I don't get you. Your advice is so damn schizophrenic. It's all over the board. In one breath you tell me how lucky I am to have this guy, that he's a freaking baby panda, and in the very next, you tell me he's no good for me and will end up breaking my heart. And you haven't even met him."

"Okay, well then let me hang out until he picks you up this afternoon, so I can meet him. Then, I can develop an informed opinion."

"No. Out of the question. Just . . . *no!*"

"And why not?"

Hannah pointed to Nicki's chest. "Ah, *hello!* You're not even wearing a bra."

"I never wear a bra."

"Yeah, well, you should."

"Get off your high horse, lady! Allow me to remind you that we both take off our clothes for a living. Yet, somehow you seem to think you're better than the rest of us."

"We're all better than the life we're living. I can't control what you or the other girls do, but I'm quitting."

"*Quitting?*"

"That's right. I'm out. I have some money saved, and I've invested wisely over the years. I'm way ahead on my mortgage and my SUV is paid for. Maybe I can get a job waitressing or something and use my savings to help make up the difference. That will give me a chance to focus on my writing. David thinks I have real talent. He believes in me. And now maybe I'm starting to believe in myself a little."

"And what are the rest of us supposed to do? You're the biggest draw at Polecats. If you quit, business will go down. That hurts all of us."

"Not my problem nor my concern. I love this guy, and I don't want to lose him over this. Don't you get that? And I love myself a lot more when I'm with him. And I loathe myself a lot more when I'm dancing at Polecats. I . . . I want to be taken seriously . . . I want to be a writer. I want to be a wife, too. And maybe one day even a mother. I don't want this life anymore. It's poison. It's prison. It's total disrespect. It's sleazy, creepy assholes who think that a twenty-dollar bill in your G-string entitles them to do whatever they want with you. There's no dignity in that. I've had it. Hashtag Me Too!"

Talking about it gave Hannah flashbacks of all the times

she'd been groped at Polecats.

"See what you've done? You've got me all worked up. I had been doing so well, too. I just took a shower and now I have to take another one."

"Scrubbing yourself raw with that damn soap-on-a-rope won't change anything. You can't wash away your past."

"You don't know how it works. It makes me feel a little cleaner. It's a survival tool, a coping mechanism."

After Nicki left, Hannah went into her bathroom and turned on the shower. As she waited for it to get hot enough, she could feel the hands on her, the hands of all the men who had fondled her. The sensation was like being touched by demons in the middle of the night, she thought.

Between the heat of the water and the heat generated by the friction of her scrubbing herself, her skin was turning red. She worried that David would notice. Examining her soap-on-a-rope, she realized she would soon need a new one. She made a mental note to order some more online. The steam from the heat filled the bathroom and hung over her like a storm cloud. As she dried herself, she sobbed because she understood her compulsion was irrational. But she still couldn't stop. *This is the definition of insanity. When you know what you're doing doesn't make any sense, but you do it anyway.*

She lay down on her bed. Within a few minutes, Rain Man negotiated his way up the pet steps that she'd placed at the foot of the bed. He staggered his way over to her, climbed on her chest, and began to knead. She gently stroked his head as he purred. He looked her in the eyes and slowly blinked. She could feel the cat's soothing powers. He extended his neck, inviting Hannah to scratch him under his chin. As she did, she closed her eyes and said a silent prayer, asking for healing.

When she finished, she opened her eyes, looked at the feline and whispered, "Do you ever pray?" He yawned. She smiled and, still whispering, continued, "I doubt you do.

Most prayers are said because someone wants or needs something. You guys don't need forgiveness for anything and you take whatever the world gives you. So there's no need for animals to pray." As she held him against her neck, he purred even louder and drifted off into a contented sleep. The landline phone rang but she didn't bother to answer. She couldn't bring herself to disturb the sleeping cat.

CHAPTER EIGHT: SEEING UNICORNS

Hannah finished packing a bit earlier than expected, so she allowed herself some time to relax. He'd be there in about an hour. She set her cell phone alarm for ten minutes before he was to arrive and took a nap on the sofa. When the alarm went off, she reached for the digital voice recorder he gave her and recorded the details of a vivid dream she'd just had. *This thing does come in handy.*

David arrived wearing a white golf shirt, a red golf cardigan, navy blue slacks, and wine colored penny loafers. He also wore a huge gold horseshoe ring encrusted with diamonds on his left ring finger. He'd stopped at a convenience store and bought them both a cup of coffee.

She had her hair up, wore jeans and a pink sweatshirt that showed a kitten floating through space in an astronaut suit. The swelling had gone down in her ankle enough that she was able to get her sneakers on both feet comfortably. She had a black and orange Orioles cap on.

"I couldn't sleep last night. I was like a little kid on Christmas Eve. I kept thinking about the evening we'd had and anticipating today," he told her.

"I know. I was pretty restless, too. I did take a little nap right before you got here. I had a very vivid dream."

"Good dream or bad dream?"

"Well, it started out bad, but it turned into something lovely. I think maybe it was an inspiration for a book. In fact, I know it was. The entire story kind of came to me in the dream. Would you like to hear it? Do we have time?"

"Sure we do. We're on vacation. There's no rush. So far as I'm concerned, we're traveling in the right-hand lane of life for the next week. Let's have our coffee and you can tell me all about it."

They sat at her kitchen table. Hannah put cream and sugar in her coffee and stirred it with a coffee stir. He was having his black.

"Oh, my God. You take yours black?"

"Ah ha. Always have."

She made a face. "Yuck. I don't see how you can drink it like that. It's so bitter."

He found his inner John Wayne and sarcastically told her, "Well, little lady, this is how a *real man* drinks his coffee. Us macho men don't go for any of those girly lattes."

She looked at him with suspicion. "I see. And I suppose all you *macho men* go to tanning salons, wear cologne that smells like a bakery, never have so much as a single hair out of place, and watch the soaps, too, huh?"

He laughed. "Point taken." He grabbed her digital voice recorder and spoke into it without actually recording. "Note to self—henceforth, do not attempt to engage Hannah in a battle of wits. She'll always win."

"Oh, how lovely. It's so nice to find one who's already been broken," she mockingly told him, as she took a sip of her coffee.

He turned serious. "Okay. You've had your fun. Now, tell me about this inspiration you've gotten. I'm dying to hear it." He leaned forward.

She took another sip of her coffee and began. "Well, it would be called *The Designated Survivors: A Love Story.*"

He nodded approval. "Good title. You already have my interest."

"Thanks . . . so it *begins* with *The End*. As in, the end of the world. Humanity finally went and did it. It destroyed itself.

Nuclear war. But right before the war starts, two people are teleported out of their beds while they sleep. The woman's name is Jennifer and she's quite beautiful and the guy's name is Matthew and he's very handsome. They wake up in a house that they've never seen before. It's just a regular house. Not fancy but not shabby either. Just a house, you know? But there are some very strange features about this house. For starters, there are intercoms set up in every room and around the property. When they wake up that first day, a voice greets them through the intercom and tells them that their world has ended and that the two of them were preselected for just such a contingency. They are the Designated Survivors and were evacuated to this small, self-contained universe known as Forever Manor. Here, they will spend Eternity, the voice tells them. Just the two of them. They'll be given all the things they need to survive. Food, water, clean clothes. Even luxury items like books, movies, and music. But it will be just the two of them. Forever. Well, needless to say, at first, they don't believe any of it. They think someone drugged them and put them in the house and is playing a very elaborate and deranged joke on them. But gradually they find out it's all true. When they walk to the edge of the property, all they can see is the blackness of space. They start to think maybe they've been kidnapped by aliens, that maybe they're some alien kid's seventh-grade science project.

"It always rains at Forever Manor. But despite all the rain, nothing ever grows. All the trees are barren, no flowers bloom, no wildlife. Everything is dead. And the house itself is freezing cold. And they can only see in black and white. There are no colors whatsoever in their world. It's a terribly depressing place to live. At the end of their lane, there's a street sign, a standard, run-of-the-mill street sign. But the name of the road that they live on is covered by a sheet of metal, which is bolted down.

"Jennifer and Matthew are very different people. He's very shy, prim and proper. He had been a librarian. She has a potty mouth and tattoos. And she's very loud and direct. At least on the surface. But deep down, she's fragile and insecure. Very smart and sensitive. And all she wants is to love and be loved. She's never had true love before. But she's harboring a terrible secret. She has a very scandalous past. She had been a *porn star—yes, a porn star—*but she's very ashamed of that and feels dirty. She thinks she took something that should be sacred—namely, sex—and made it profane.

"She starts to fall in love with Matthew because he's very sweet and kind and gentle and she's never had that before. He starts to fall in love with her, too. And one day, right before they are getting ready to kiss, she tells him about her past. Because she wants to be honest with him. But he rejects her and tells her that he could never be with someone like her, someone who's done what she's done, someone who's tainted. She's crushed and concludes that Forever Manor must surely be Hell itself, because Hell, to her at least, is the impossibility of love. For all Eternity, she's condemned to live a loveless life.

"When he rejects her, a terrible tempest starts outside. Sheets of rain, hail, hurricane force winds. Lightning is hurled from the heavens. She runs outside into the storm and throws herself down in the mud and sobs and wishes she was dead.

"The voice speaks to Matthew through the intercom and tells him that he had the power to set her free but instead chose to imprison her by refusing to love her. Matthew tells the voice that he can forgive her but can't forget about her past. The voice tells him that forgetting is part of forgiving and that you can't forgive unless you forget, too.

"The voice then reads Matthew a poem Jennifer wrote called *Happy Endings*. It's a melancholy poem about a woman who can never have a happy ending because the man that she loves won't love her back. It's such a sad little poem and she bares her soul in it. And it moves Matthew and he sees that her heart is pure, even if her body isn't. He rushes out into the storm and finds her and throws himself down in the mud with her. They're both covered in mud, you know? And she's sobbing so hard and tells him to leave her alone. He caresses her cheek and tells her that he loves her and that he was wrong. He tells her that he was foolish and arrogant and self-righteous and pigheaded. He kisses her, and she kisses him back. And slowly, color starts to come into their world. It flickers on and off at first. But as their kiss becomes more passionate, it finally comes on and stays on. And the colors are more real and vibrant than anything the human eye has ever seen. Then the storm suddenly stops, the clouds part and the sun comes out. A rainbow forms. Then, everything that was dead starts coming to life. In the blink of an eye, flowers and trees bloom to reveal a beautiful garden. Wildlife appears in the yard. The coldness of Forever Manor is replaced by a gentle warmth. Jennifer is filthy from rolling around in the mud, but she's never felt cleaner in her life.

"See the irony there? She's literally dirty but figuratively clean. She tells Matthew that she loves him, too, and they kiss some more. And they can see, off in the distance, that the storm blew the sheet metal off the sign and the name of their street is now visible. Hand-in-hand they walk up to the sign and look at it. And everything suddenly makes sense. The sign reads . . . *Eden Way*. They kiss again and hold each other tight and a chorus of angels appear in the sky and serenade them with *What A Wonderful World*. You see, all along, they've been in the Garden of Eden. But Eden couldn't be Eden—Paradise couldn't be Paradise—until love was present. Because nothing can grow, thrive or prosper without love. Entire worlds pass away for want of love. But once love bloomed, so did everything else in their world. Love transformed everything.

"God had just enough grace left in His heart to let humanity start over. He made a New Heaven and a New Earth, just like it says in the Book of Revelation. And Matthew and Jennifer are the New Adam and the New Eve. And they lived happily ever after. The End.

"Of course, there's a lot more to it. This is just kind of a synopsis. I think it would either be a short story or a novella; not enough characters for a full-scale novel. What do you think? I want a totally honest opinion."

He wiped his eyes. "I think you must have some onions sitting around somewhere."

"So are you saying that my story moved you?"

He nodded. "If that story doesn't touch your soul, then you don't have one."

She clapped her hands. "Yes! That's what I was going for. Like I told you at Tiffany's, I want to move people with my stories. That's what a writer is supposed to do."

He got up and walked over to her side of the table. "Can you stand up, or does it hurt too much?"

"No, no. I can stand. I can actually put a little weight on it for short periods of time now." She gingerly got up. They stood inches apart. He looked at her with total adoration.

"Oh, ah, should I turn my cap around and put it on backward again? Is this the part where I'm supposed to do that?" she asked.

"Please."

She turned it around and smiled up at him. "You know, if it's more convenient, I could stop wearing ball caps."

"No way. You've got to represent. Besides, it's kind of fun turning it around. Adds to the excitement and anticipation."

She raised her eyebrows. "So it's kind of like foreplay?"

"Yeah, you could say that. A very G-rated version of foreplay." He put his finger under her chin and she instinctively tilted her head up. He gave her a passionate, open mouth kiss and his hands took a trip down south. When he got to the small of her back, he kept going and crossed the border. Finally, he settled on her ass. He briefly squeezed it and she let out a little gasp of pleasure.

After she vocalized, he quickly moved his hands up to her shoulders and broke off the kiss. "Gosh, I'm sorry! I didn't mean to touch you on your backside. I got caught up in the moment. God, I can't believe I did that!" He smacked himself in the forehead with his open palm, then continued, "I don't know what got into me. I just—"

She looked at him and pressed her index finger to his lips before he could say anything more. "Hush and listen to me for a second, okay?" she told him. He nodded. "Being a gentleman is wonderful. Don't get me wrong—I'm not complaining. I *want* a gentleman. But sometimes, you can be too much of a gentleman. Understand?"

"No. I'm lost in fact. What are you saying?"

"I'm saying that I want us to move beyond the G-rated stuff. I'm saying I want you to touch me like that. I . . . I want to give myself to you and I want you to give yourself to me. Do you know what I mean by that? Do you understand what I'm getting at?"

"I think so."

"Well, then tell me, so I know that we're both on the same page."

He took a deep breath. "Okay. You're talking about making love."

"That's right. And how do you feel about that?"

He looked her up and down and nodded. "I want to make love to you. I want to be as close to you as possible. I want that more than anything else in the world."

"You don't have a problem with people having sex prior to marriage?"

He looked up at the ceiling and let out a sigh and laughed a nervous laugh. "I knew that question was going to rear its ugly head. Look, if two people care for one another, there's no sin in the physical expression of that caring. It depends on whether the sex is in the context of a loving, committed relationship. A lot of people would say I'm wrong, but I don't think I am. I think God is glad anytime two of His children treat one another with tenderness."

"That's exactly what I said. Almost verbatim. I said the very same thing when I was talking to Nicki."

"It sounds like we're on the same page, huh?"

"It does. What do you think about us making love at the ocean?" she asked.

"That's about as romantic as it gets."

"Exactly. So can we plan on that?"

"Yeah. Definitely. And, for the record, you don't think I'm a cad for touching your . . . ah . . . for touching your . . ."

"Ass," she said, filling in the blank for him. She paused, flashed a naughty smile and wiggle her butt from side to side. "My sugarshaker. Isn't that what they call it down South?"

"Yeah, what you said." He blushed.

She rolled her eyes. "Come a little closer," she told him. He inched forward until he could feel her breasts against his chest.

She took his hands in hers and squeezed them. Then she kissed him and during the kiss took his hands and placed them on her backside. This time, he allowed himself to explore. He squeezed, massaged, and even playfully smacked that ass.

When they finally broke the kiss, she whispered to him,

"God, I want to make love to you. I don't know if I can wait. I want to take you into my bedroom right now and make love to you. I'm very horny."

His hands were still on her ass. "I feel the same way, but we should wait until we get to the ocean."

"Why? Tell me why?"

"Because of pro wrestling."

"*Excuse me?*" she folded her arms and looked at him with agitation. "Oh, this has to be one doozy of a simile. *Romance is like pro wrestling because* . . . So let's hear it, bub."

"Well, now, give me a chance, here. See, when I was a kid, I loved pro wrestling. When you go to a wrestling show, they never start with the main event. You have a series of preliminary matches, and everything builds to the main event. It builds . . . and it builds, and it builds, you see? That sense of anticipation makes the whole show better."

"So our relationship is like professional wrestling? May I remind you, sir, that pro wrestling is fake."

"Okay, as a wrestling fan, I have to correct you. Like Ric Flair always says *it's not fake, it's choreographed.*"

She shot him a look of agitation. He continued, "And here's the thing—pro wrestling storylines always have happy endings. The good guys always win. The bad guys ultimately get their comeuppance. Good always defeats evil. There's always a happily-ever-after in wrestling."

"Well, I'll have to take your word for it because I've never been a fan myself. But when I finally do have you, I'll be good to you. I promise."

"I feel very blessed. I found a smart, sweet, kind, sexy woman. Someone who I can talk literature or old movies or baseball with and then make love to." He kissed her on the forehead.

She closed her eyes and was breathing heavy. "Okay, we need to change the subject, like, *right now* because if we don't—if you keep talking like that—I'm going to jump your bones right here. And I'm quite serious about that."

"Well, let's talk about Bobby and Babs and where we're at with them," he said.

"I emailed the Finally Free Foundation, told them all about the conditions at the zoo. They would like as much documentation as possible, so I thought when we stop by today, we should get some video. They seem like they're sincerely interested," she said.

"Good. I talked to my friend down at the television station and he said they'll try to do a story on it. I've got the social media pages up and running. We're making some progress."

"Part of me hates to go there because it breaks my heart and it brings me down. And today of all days, I don't want to be brought down. But Bobby and Babs are counting on us. Right now, we're the only advocates they have in the entire world. And if this doesn't work, then they're condemned to spend the rest of their lives pacing in that tiny, filthy little cage," she said.

"I know." He kissed her tenderly on the head. "But this will work. They *will* be free. And they'll roar. And they'll have a beautiful cub together."

"I believe you."

He turned her cap back around for her. "You know, if you wore your cap backward in public, you might actually start a new trend. I think you'd suddenly see every woman in Baltimore doing it. They'd even come up with an official term for it, they'd call it the Tomboy Turnaround. You'd be like the Baltimore version of Jackie O."

"So I could be a trendsetter, huh?"

"Most definitely."

"Well, while we're on the topic of fashion trends, Liberace called, and he wants his ring back." She playfully brushed the tip of his nose with her finger.

He looked at his ring. "You don't like my ring?"

"I was just teasing."

"I mean, I know not all of us can have the impeccable taste that you have, but I do my best. I . . . I thought it looked good, classy even. But I guess I don't know what class is." He looked down at the ring and shook his head.

"I didn't mean anything by it. It was supposed to be a joke more than anything. Sometimes, couples do that, you know? They poke fun at one another in a good-natured way."

He slyly grinned. "You've been a bad girl, a naughty girl, and now you need a good spanking." He grabbed her by the waist and put his hand on her behind and lightly spanked her.

"Oh, you're awful. Here you let me think I had really offended you. You're ornery, is what you are."

He cackled, proud that he had fooled her, as he continued to spank her lightly. He did his best imitation of a wrestling commentator. "Oh, look at this, wrestling fans! The Minister of Mayhem is applying his patented move, *The Atomic Sugarshaker Smackaroo*, to that feisty little filly!" She squealed with delight. And then they kissed again.

After a few minutes, he reluctantly told her, "I guess we should, you know, head out to the zoo."

"Yeah. I guess."

"To be continued."

She emphatically nodded. "To be continued."

"I'm packed up. I guess we can load up the car now," she said.

"I'll carry all your stuff out for you."

They would load up, stop at the zoo and then swing back to their respective homes to pick up Brandi and Rain Man.

She had a black guitar case set out with the rest of her

luggage.

"You play guitar?"

"Yeah. You don't mind if I bring it, do you? I mean, if there's not enough room in the trunk, I can leave it."

"There's plenty of room in that trunk. Do you promise to play me something? I'll bet you sing, too, right?" he asked.

She shrugged her shoulders. "Well, right or wrong, I sing."

"I would love it if you would play something for me that has special meaning to you. Would you do that?"

"I will."

"Wonderful. I already have two things to look forward to."

When they got to the zoo, he handed her a packet of tissues.

"Now, did you just happen to have those in your pocket or did you purposely pick them up this morning knowing this place makes me cry?"

He didn't say anything. He didn't have to. She knew.

She took the tissues from him and unwrapped them. "Awfully sweet of you. Those little gestures really do matter. We women notice those things." They smiled at one another.

He placed his arm around her as they approached the lions' enclosure. Bobby and Babs were pacing. Bobby's coat was in very bad shape. It was dull and there were large bald patches. Babs' limp had gotten worse. Both cats looked very thin.

"They look so defeated. It's as if they've accepted this hell as their lot in life," she said.

They both took out their phones and started recording.

David looked at them and shook his head. "They're living in misery. And for what? So that us humans can gawk at them and old man Rupert can charge us for the privilege.

And yet they still claim that humanity is the most highly evolved form of life on the planet. Truth is, animals live closer to God than most people ever will. I mean, think about it—they don't hate, their love is unconditional. And they're extremely forgiving. Why, look at little Brandi. Her previous person poured chemicals on her back. But she still loves everyone."

Her eyes lit up with inspiration. "Hey! Just got an idea. How about your church? Would your church lend a hand with Bobby and Babs?" she asked.

He laughed. "Are you kidding me? Bishop Higgins, my supervisor, doesn't like animals. I recently got in trouble with him over my approving Church funds for a cat's medication. And he had a fit about me bringing Brandi to Sunday morning services to make a point about not judging."

"Then I feel sorry for him. I feel sorry for anyone who doesn't know what it's like to feel an animal's love."

He again laughed. "Maybe you should be the priest. You'd be a better one than I am. You see, I'd like to pity Bishop Higgins—I would. But he's such an example of a walking pile of shit that I find it difficult to care."

She was mildly taken aback. "That's the first time I've heard you curse. Granted, that was pretty mild. But this Higgins character—he's really that bad?"

"Yep. I think his theology is that God is synonymous with control. But God doesn't want to control anything, you know? Like in *The Designated Survivors*. God didn't bring about Armageddon. Humanity did. And God didn't force Matthew to love Jennifer. It was up to Matthew to make that choice. It's all about options. And having the freedom to exercise those options. But I don't think the bishop views it that way. To him, God's a tyrant, not a liberator."

"He sounds miserable."

"Have you ever looked at someone and wondered why

they're doing the job that they're doing?"

Every day when I look in the mirror. "I guess some people aren't cut out for the work that they end up doing."

"Amen. And Miles Higgins is definitely in the wrong profession. He has no business being a priest."

"I'm sorry you have to deal with someone like that."

"He's one of the reasons I question more and more whether I am in the right line of work."

"Do you still think you'd like to be a baseball announcer?"

"Yeah, I do. I can find more of God on a baseball diamond than I can in your average church. I don't know if that's more of a testament to the greatness of sports or a condemnation of organized religion."

As they watched Bobby drink from a bowl of dirty water, she held his hand and put her head on his shoulder.

"I'm going to start writing. Because I think . . . no, I *know* that I'm in the wrong profession," she said.

"The hostess thing, you mean?"

"Yeah. The hostess thing."

"Well, after hearing the synopsis for your first book, I have to say it would be a sin if you didn't focus on your writing. You have real talent. I'm not just saying that, either."

She turned to him, put both arms around his waist and smiled up at him.

"Penny for your thoughts," he said.

She whispered. "I was thinking that before this day is through, I'm going to make love to you. And anticipating that fills my soul with an electricity. And it . . . makes me . . . wet."

"Wet? It's not raining."

She rolled her eyes. "Please tell me that was a joke. You can't be that naïve."

"It wasn't one of my better zingers."

"So what's your favorite part of the female anatomy?"

"Aw, I don't know. I like it all."

"Oh, please. I don't want to hear the yearbook answer. That's bullshit. I want a *real* answer."

He nodded. "Okay. Fair enough. I like boobs. So there. There you have it. I can admit it. I'm a boob man."

She smiled and nodded. "You are, are you?"

"Yeah. I once sat through an entire episode of *Keeping up with the Kardashians* just to see Kim in a bikini top. That's a pretty big sacrifice just to see some cleavage." He smirked at her.

"Wonderful. See, that's an honest answer. That's what I was looking for. And, ah, I think you'll be very pleased with what I bring to the table in that area."

"Right. I could kind of tell that first time that we were dancing in the diner that you're pretty stacked." He paused, looked up and said, "God, I feel so embarrassed saying that."

"Why would you feel embarrassed?"

"Because I'm a priest. I'm not supposed to talk like that."

"You were a man before you were a priest. And you're still a man first and foremost. That doesn't mean that God can't use you. Just that He'll have to share you. With me. But it should be at least a ninety-ten split, in my favor. Because He has an entire legion of angels. And you're the only one that I have."

"That's the nicest thing anyone has ever said about me, but I'm not an angel."

"Neither am I. We're all, to varying degrees, a combination of good and bad."

"That may be true, but I'd still vote you *Most Likely To See A Unicorn*."

She looked at him with suspicion. "What in the world are

you talking about?"

"Well, according to legend, only the pure of heart can see unicorns."

She reached around to put her hand on his ass and whispered to him. "Yeah? Well, there's nothing pure about the thoughts that I'm having right now. You wait until I get you behind closed doors . . ."

"Oh yeah?" he asked.

"Oh, *yeah*," she barked back at him in a husky, sultry voice.

He launched into his televangelist impression. "Well, in that case, I'm going to prophesy that the Spirit will soon move me to lay hands on you, sister! Woo! Hal-lay-lou-ya!" They both giggled like teenagers.

They said goodbye to Bobby and Babs. Both cats were still incessantly pacing. Hannah again cried. "It literally hurts my soul to leave them like this," she told him.

As they walked to the car, they saw the zoo staff preparing a new exhibit. They had affixed a fake horn to the forehead of a white mare named Abigail. A sign advertised her as *The World's Only Unicorn Held in Captivity.*

CHAPTER NINE: LOVING YOU

As they crossed the Chesapeake Bay Bridge, Hannah looked over her shoulder into the back seat. "Aw. The kids look so cute. Rain Man's sucking on his little stuffed elephant that I put in his carrier and Brandi is sleeping on her back with all four feet in the air." She sank back in her seat feeling content, feeling like the four of them made up a kind of blended family. And that made her happy.

He asked her to open the glove box and take out a cassette tape. She pulled it out, examined it, and read the album title aloud. "*Sounds of the Seventies*, huh?"

With tortoiseshell Ray Ban sunglasses on, he briefly glanced over at her. "Yeah. It's a good album. It was in the glovebox when I bought the car from an estate sale. Back in nineteen ninety-seven, when this baby rolled off the assembly line, cassette players were still standard."

Hannah handed him the tape and he inserted it into the tape deck. Badfinger's *Day After Day* played. She listened intently and said, "Oh, wow. Pretty song."

"I know, right? Some great music came out of the seventies." He started to sing along softly.

She turned sideways in the passenger seat, as much as she could, given that she was wearing her seatbelt and trying her best to protect her ankle. She blurted out, "McDonald's or Burger King?"

He stopped singing and took his eyes off the road long enough to flash her an incredulous look. "Huh?"

She shrugged her shoulders and repeated herself.

"McDonald's or Burger King? I want to know all I can about you. It's a very basic matter of preference and it says a lot about a person. I'm curious about which camp you're in. I don't think it's an unreasonable question."

He laughed. "Okay, if you really must know — neither. I'm a Waffle House man."

"Waffle House?"

He nodded. "Absolutely. Remember, I went to school in Tennessee and Waffle House is huge down there. And their pecan waffles are to die for."

"I've never even been inside a Waffle House," she sheepishly admitted.

"Oh yeah? Well, if you want to talk about an impressive *never*, I can top that. I've never used an ATM," he proudly announced.

She made a face. "Oh! Weird. Why not?"

"You need a personal identification number to use them. Life already has too many damn PINs. I refuse to be encumbered by any more. My boycott of ATMs is my way of protesting. I refuse to put any more PINs in my head. I won't become another PIN head."

"That sounds like something Kramer from *Seinfeld* would rant about," she observed.

He thought for a moment and said, "It does, doesn't it?" They both laughed.

They stopped at a red light and he took his hands off the steering wheel, stretched his arms and casually asked, "Do you have any other weird *nevers*?"

She thought for a moment, took a miniature candy bar from her purse, and unwrapped it. Holding it up, she announced, "Leftover from last Halloween. Found a whole bag of them hiding in the back of my Lazy Susan. Hope they're still good." She tentatively took a bite. With the candy in her mouth, she said, "Well, I've never taken a Hanukkah gift, or any other gift for that matter, back to the store for exchange. I think it's rude and it totally defeats the spirit in which gifts are given. I mean, if someone cares enough to give you a gift, just accept it. Be happy with it, even if you're not crazy about the color, style, brand or whatever. You know?"

"I don't take gifts back to stores to exchange them, either," he told her.

"Really?"

"Yeah. If I don't like a gift, I approach the person who gave it and ask for the receipt . . . so I can get the cash." He guffawed, glanced at her and winked.

She reached over and playfully smacked his wrist. "Smart ass."

He turned serious. "I was teasing. I agree with you. I think what you just said—it's a wonderful sentiment. The world would be a better place if people could learn to want what they have, instead of trying to figure out how to have everything they want."

She nodded agreement, put the last piece of the candy bar in her mouth, and closed the heater vent on the passenger side. "Okay. One more question. And this is a fun one. Jennifer Lawrence or Jennifer Lopez? Or maybe Jennifer Love Hewitt?"

He stopped laughing and a serious look crossed his face. Reaching over the center console, he held her hand and gently squeezed it. "None of the above. I'm not into Hollywood starlets. I'm into sexy tomboys."

He put the car in park, unbuckled his seat belt, leaned across the cabin and kissed her. The light turned green and the cars behind them started honking their horns. As he put his seatbelt back on, he looked into the rearview mirror and noticed that he had a little smudge of chocolate on his lips. "That was definitely one sweet kiss," he told her.

They made good time. By late afternoon, they had arrived at the Diocesan house, an old, elegant, cobalt blue Victorian house right on the ocean. She hobbled out of the car and took it in.

"Oh, this is gorgeous. And it's huge."

"Well, they use it for workshops and such. Hey, shouldn't you be using your crutches?"

"Oh, I can put weight on it for short periods of time. It really is healing." She took in a deep breath. "The air at the ocean always has this . . . this amazing quality to it. I swear it relaxes you, like a natural tranquilizer."

"This would be a good place for you to start writing. At night, you could sit in one of the upstairs bedrooms with the window open and write away. The sound of the waves crashing ashore might stimulate your imagination."

"Maybe tomorrow. We kind of have a date tonight, right?" She raised her eyebrows and smiled.

"Right." He blushed.

They got Brandi and Rain Man set up inside and went to check out the boardwalk. He tried to get her to use one of the motorized courtesy carts that the Chamber of Commerce provided for disabled visitors, but she declined and told him, "I'll do just fine. I don't want to take a cart from someone who needs one more than me."

As they walked past Artie's Arcade, they saw an automated fortuneteller named Madam Doria. She had been set up just inside the entrance. If you inserted a dollar bill into her bill validator, she would prophesy one's future. Hannah thought she looked downright spooky, like a nineteenth-century parlor medium, one who was more than capable of conjuring up some evil spirits and plenty of bad mojo when the mood struck her. Nonetheless, David insisted on stopping and giving it a go. "Just for kicks," he told her.

He put his dollar in and they waited. Creepy music

played, and Madam Doria opened her eerie mechanical brown doe eyes. Her crystal ball lit up and she tilted her head forward and peered into it. In a robotic, feminine voice that poorly attempted to recreate an Eastern European accent, she quickly spat out her prognostication. "In the near future, you will visit a wild and exotic place." Her crystal ball went dim and she raised her head back to its original position. She closed her eyes and waited for her computer chip to notify her that it was time to spit out a new, vague premonition to the next paying customer. David got a thoughtful look on his face and squinted his eyes, trying to decipher the message. "Wild and exotic? Wild and exotic . . ." he said. Suddenly, he snapped his fingers. "Hey! I got it! Next month I have to renew my license at the DMV. Last time I was there, someone took a dump in the urinal, put porn magazines on the magazine exchange table, and there was a befuddled gent who couldn't understand why a car with a tiller instead of a steering wheel couldn't pass inspection. I'd say that's pretty darn *wild and exotic*." He laughed at his own joke. Hannah rolled her eyes and shook her head.

As they walked along the boardwalk, she took in a deep breath. "Wow. You have to love the smell of the boardwalk. You get this incredible aroma, a combination of sea salt, taffy, French fries, cotton candy, hotdogs, and pizza. I think some perfume mogul should make a fragrance that combines all those scents and call it *Boardwalk*."

Putt-Putt Patty's, a miniature golf course, had just opened for the season. When they walked by, she noticed that he kept looking over at it.

"You like miniature golf?" she asked.

"I like golf period. Most ex-ballplayers do. It's a sport that allows you to exercise your competitive nature long after your playing days are over. I have my own clubs and play at Turf Valley on Saturdays in the summer."

She got a mischievous smile on her face. "You know, you look like you could be a golf pro."

"You think?"

"Oh, yeah, baby." She licked her lips. "And I can't wait to see your nine iron."

He turned beet red. She reached up and pinched his cheek. "Aw, shy guy. My shy guy." He smiled and nodded, and her pinch transitioned to a gentle caress of his cheek

They stopped at Frank's Pizza for dinner and had meatball parmesan sandwiches and steak fries. They ate outside, at the picnic tables that offered a view of the ocean. They were close enough that they could hear the surf. A few seagulls gathered near the tables and scarfed up scraps offered by the customers. They laughed when one large gull swooped down and stole a small piece of pizza off someone's plate and flew off with it.

She sipped on her orange soda, then asked, "So when's the last time you had sex?"

"A long time."

"How long?"

He let out an agitated sigh. "I don't see why this is important."

"I think I have a right to know."

He took a deep breath. "Since before I became a priest."

"You've been a priest for, what, two years now?"

"That's right."

"Tell me about her."

"Look, this is awkward."

She shook her head. "Doesn't have to be. I'm not going to judge anything."

"All right. But it was a bit of a crazy scenario. See, when I was playing ball, me and some of my buddies flew out to Vegas during the New York Penn League All-Star break. I met a woman in a bar and she was pretty. Not as pretty as you, mind you, but she was pretty. And she asked me to go home with her, said we could listen to music."

She interrupted him and shook her head like a fighter trying to clear the cobwebs after being knocked down. "Wait. You fell for that? You fell for the *let's go back to my place to listen to music* line?

"Ah-ha. I didn't know it was a line at the time."

She took a deep breath. "Okay. Continue."

"Yeah, well, anyhow, when we got back to her place, you know, she became pretty aggressive. She knew I was a ballplayer. She kept telling me that she wanted me to hit her a *touchdown* with that *big bat* of mine. Well, I tried to explain to her that she didn't even have her terminology right, that you hit home runs in baseball and score touchdowns in football."

She laughed. "What did she say to that?"

"Her exact words were *what-the-fuck-ever, Howard Cosell!* I tried to tell her that we should get to know each other better, that I didn't feel right having sex with her because we had just met. She told me that if I wasn't going to have sex with her, that I had to get out of her house and find my own way back to my hotel. Well, she lived in Henderson, which is about twenty miles from the Strip. I didn't have much money on me and at that time didn't even own a credit card, so I was screwed. Literally."

"So she basically blackmailed you?"

"I guess you could say that. I mean, she didn't force herself on me or anything, but she kind of used my fear against me. She told me that it was just sex. After it was over, she said *you're a guy, you're supposed to want it all the time. Why were you so reluctant to screw me?* Well, I looked at her, looked her right in her eyes, right in her pretty doe eyes, and I said *because, maybe, just maybe, I thought you could be worth more than a one-night stand.*"

"And what did she say to that?"

"She started crying and said she was sorry. She asked me

to hold her, so I did. Then she took me back to my hotel room. We kept in touch for a little while but, ah, I haven't talked to her in years. I ended up feeling sorry for her. She didn't have love in her life. Lots of sex, but no love. And she was treating me the way guys had treated her—not that that made it right—but that's what she was doing. She was pathetic, and I mean that in the literal sense of the word, not as a pejorative. Told you it was crazy. But, hey, life is crazy sometimes, you know? That's how it happened."

She reached across the table and put her hand on top of his. "Well, I promise, tonight won't be crazy unless it's crazy in a good way." She thought a moment, then added, "What you said to her was wonderful, though. You granted her more worth and dignity than she granted to herself. There's a real beauty in that and I suspect she understood that, which is why she cried. You're a beautiful person. Inside and out. And that matters." He leaned across the table and kissed her.

When they got back to the house, she got her guitar. It had a *sunburst* finish, and she had affixed a rainbow sticker to its body. They went into the backyard just in time for Twilight. He put down a blanket and built a fire in the fire ring, then got out two beers from a cooler and tuned his phone to pick up the Orioles game.

"Want a beer?" he asked, then added, "I figured a tomboy would rather have a beer over some frilly wine cooler."

"Good thinking. I'm definitely a beer girl, though I rarely drink at all. But tonight's special."

"That's how I see it, too. Tonight's special."

They clinked their dark, glass bottles together in a toast and sipped on the beer while Mother Nature provided the entertainment. In the Atlantic, the dark blue water contrasted with the dark orange of the horizon and bright yellow-orange of the sun. A dolphin leaped from the water and she was tickled by it because she had never seen that, except on TV.

"What do you think about the view?" he asked.

"I feel power, raw power. Power easily capable of being extremely violent, if it so chose. But tonight, it's chosen to be peaceful. It's quite surreal actually."

"Almost as if this is some strange, foreign place," he suggested.

"Yes. Exactly. Something in between Heaven and Earth. I feel like I'm returning to somewhere I've never been to before. It gives me chills."

As the sun prepared to go off duty, it morphed colors and took on the appearance of a giant tunnel of brilliant white light. Then they saw the big finish, the showstopper. As it dipped below the horizon, it briefly acquired a green halo — a green flash sunset. They sat there in silence and then turned to gaze into each other's eyes. And they listened to the rhythm of the ocean.

Finally, he said, "That sunset was your opening act. Why don't you go ahead and play your guitar for me?"

She nervously laughed. "That's a heck of an opening act to follow."

"You can do it. I totally believe in you."

"I'm not some musical superstar," she said.

With mock melodrama he told her, "You don't have to be a star, baby, to play in my show."

She rolled her eyes and shook her head. "Oh, God, okay. Let's get this over with." She picked up her guitar and tuned the strings.

"What are you going to play for me?"

"My own song. I wrote it myself. It's called *Caged Lions Never Roar*."

He leaned forward and recorded her with his phone as she strummed the guitar and sang the melancholy song, a tribute to Bobby and Babs. And more. The chorus went—

Inside, They're Dyin'/There's Nothing Sadder Than a Silent Lion
But When Freedom's Taken Away/There's Nothing Left To Say
Caged Lions Never Roar/Caged Lions Want So Much More
Caged Lions Just Want To Be Free/Caged Lions Are Just Like Me

When she finished, she waited for his reaction. There was utter silence, save for the sounds of the surf crashing into the beach.

Finally, he said, "That was lovely, Hannah. Lovely. Thank you for sharing that with me. You have a pretty voice."

"I want to share more than a song with you. I want to share myself with you," she said.

It was getting chilly with the sun now down.

"Maybe we should head inside. Are you cold?" he asked.

"It's a little chilly, but I want to do one more thing before we go in." She delicately got up and motioned for him to get up as well.

"Dance with me," she said.

"Is your ankle strong enough?"

"If it starts hurting, we'll do what we did at Tiffany's. Because I know you'll never let me fall. Right?"

He nodded. "Right."

She pulled her phone from her back pocket and put her arms around his neck. Looking over his shoulder, she used the light of the fire to scroll through her music and made her selection. She picked Elvis' *Loving You*, telling him, "I love Elvis. There was never any harm in Elvis."

They swayed back and forth. Eventually, her ankle started hurting, so he lifted her up and she wrapped her legs around his waist and they kissed. And the only sounds they could hear was the voice of a young Elvis Presley singing those tender, gentle words and the waves fulfilling their destiny.

When the song ended, they locked eyes and she said, with great conviction, "Loving you."

"I know. It's a beautiful song. I like Elvis, too. Especially his early stuff, before he became a prisoner of his own fame."

"I'm not talking about the song. I wasn't referring to a song title." Then she whispered, "Loving *you* . . . loving *you*." She watched intently and waited for him to absorb and process her words.

He took a deep breath and kissed her with his eyes. "Can't help falling in love," he softly told her, as he brushed her blonde hair away from her eyes with his hand. Then he added, "And I wasn't referencing a song either."

A full moon shone down on them—like a spotlight. And she wondered if maybe, just maybe, they were the stars of that night's picture show in Heaven.

He doused the fire in the fire ring and they went inside. The bedrooms were upstairs.

"How's that ankle holding out?"

"Hurts a little. Not too bad."

He scooped her up in his arms.

"You're going to carry me, are you?"

"Of course. You're not climbing those stairs on that ankle."

She placed her arms around his neck. "It's good to have someone to take care of you," she noted.

Brandi and Rain Man were napping together, on the living room sofa. Rain Man had reached out a paw and put it on the Pitbull's back. They were both roused by the creaky floorboards on the stairs and went to follow David and Hannah.

Hannah gently admonished them. "Guys, mommy and daddy need some private time to do the things mommies and daddies do together." Both animals nonetheless followed them up the stairs. He carried her into the master bedroom, closed the door before Rain Man and Brandi could get in, and gently set her down on the bed. It was a large bedroom with a huge king-sized bed. He sat down next to her.

As soon as he sat down, he popped right back up. He snapped his fingers and said, "Oh, check this out. You're going to love this." He went to the closet and pulled out an old lava lamp, plugged it in and turned it on.

"Pretty cool, huh?" he asked.

She frowned and shook her head. "No. No to the lava lamp."

"No? Really?"

"Really. It's something a nineteen seventies' gigolo would have had in his bedroom."

"Okay. No lava lamp . . . Hey! Do you want to see my baseball card collection? I brought it to show you. I have some cards from the fifties. They're worth *a lot* of money."

She again shook her head, this time very emphatically. "No. No baseball cards."

"Fortnite? Some Fortnite?"

"No."

She patted the bed. "Come over here and sit down next to me."

"Sure. Give me a minute." He stood at attention, placed his right hand over his heart, and started singing the Star-Spangled Banner. He wasn't singing it well, either.

She interrupted. "Okay there Francis Scott Off-Key, what's this all about?"

He stopped and told her, "Every important event starts with The National Anthem. Now, will you show some respect, please?" He motioned for her to stand. She rolled her eyes at him but nonetheless stood and placed her hand over her heart until he was finished.

Then he sat down and twiddled his thumbs before asking, "Know what really burns me up? When you get to a fast food joint, like, two minutes before they start serving lunch and they still will only take breakfast orders. That five-minute window between breakfast and lunch—that's *no man's land.* They should be willing to take both breakfast and lunch orders during that time. But will they? No! That happened to me the other week and I don't mind telling you, I was peeved. I didn't even reciprocate the cashier's *have a nice day* when I left."

She let out a deep sigh, blew lip bubbles, crossed her arms, and looked up at the ceiling. "You, brute, you."

"I'm thinking about writing to the CEO. And don't think I won't because I will."

"I'm sure they'll send you a coupon for a free burger and fries," she sarcastically told him.

He ignored her sarcasm. "You think?"

She wagged her finger at him. "Here's what I think. I think *you're* nervous."

"Me? Nervous? Listen, baby, I've got nerves of steel. I did play two seasons of Class A minor league baseball, after all."

"It takes nerve to play *minor* league baseball, huh?" She made a face and stuck out her tongue.

"Sure it does. Some of those motels we had to stay in—well, let's just say you never knew what you might possibly catch from sleeping on those bed sheets."

She flashed him a scowl.

Finally, he nodded. "Okay—okay, so I'm a little nervous. I want this to be perfect. Perfect for you. That, and it's been a while, a long while, since I've been, ah, you know, intimate with anyone."

She scooted up the bed until she was near the pillows. "Here, I want you to stretch out and put your head in my lap." He did and looked up at her as she ran her hand along his cheek.

She spoke to him in a gentle whisper. "Don't be nervous, okay?"

He nodded.

"David, making love — truly making love — it can be liberating. But only if you let it. So let it. Okay?"

"Okay."

She smiled at him and said, "And just like you promised to never hurt me, I promise to never, ever hurt you."

"I know that. I trust you."

She motioned for him to lift his head and she got up and pushed him down on the bed until he was lying flat on his back. Then she climbed on top of him and started kissing him and she reached down with one hand and placed her hand on his crotch. She could tell he was already very hard for her. She whispered, "Good boy. Very good. You're relaxing. We're going to make each other feel *really, really* good tonight."

She started pulling his sweater up. "Let's get these clothes off you." When she took off his shirt, she pressed her cheek against his tanned, hairless chest and kissed it. Then she pulled his pants off, and finally his boxers.

"No tan lines. So you tan in the nude, huh?"

He nodded.

"I like your body," she told him. "And your penis is just right. Big but not grotesquely big. I think you really are playing with a nine iron." He turned an even deeper shade of red. She laughed. "Aw, shy guy. My shy guy. There's so much pushiness in this world. That shyness of yours is the perfect antidote. It's very endearing."

"Thanks." That was the only word he could muster.

"Why don't you help me undress now?"

He pulled her sweatshirt off and examined the graphic on

the front. "That design's funny—a cat as an astronaut. Because cats can't really be astronauts," he said. She giggled. Then he pulled off her jeans. She was wearing a matching black satin bra and panty set. Her breasts were even larger than he had imagined.

He looked at her right wrist and she still had her soap around it. He went to slip it off. She stopped him.

"Let's leave that on, honey, okay?"

"You want to leave it on even while we're making love?" he asked.

"Yes, I have to. I can't be without it."

He looked confused. "I thought it was just a silly good luck charm."

"It's a little more. I'll tell you about it later, okay? But for now, indulge me. Please."

"Sure. Sure. It's not a huge deal."

I hope you feel the same way when I tell you everything. "Thank you, David."

He took off her bra and tentatively reached up and gently squeezed her breasts. "I like your boobies." He caressed them and philosophized. "I don't know why these things are so much fun, but they are. They're kind of like fidget spinners and Slinkys. Simple concept but they'll keep you entertained for hours."

After a few moments, he turned his attention to her panties. She stopped him. "Hold off on that. I'm going to give you a special treat. Here, sit up and lean back against the headboard." He complied.

She straddled him, put her arms around him and performed a modified lap dance, grinding hard on him. Moving her hips back and forth, side to side in a smooth, seamless motion. Then, she began moving on him in a very slow, deliberate, circular motion. She bit her lower lip and looked him in the eyes, trying to convey all her love.

He was breathing heavy. He reached up and caressed her golden hair. "God, your hair feels like silk." Reaching down, he ran his hands along her legs. "And your legs do, too. I love your legs. They're so smooth and shiny."

She pressed against his crotch hard. "I need to be closer to you. I need you inside me."

He helped her off with her panties. "I adore you," he said and reached up, kissed her on the forehead, then wrapped his arms around her. She put her arms around him. And they held that position for the longest time, exchanging body heat in a drafty old house on a chilly night.

He heard her start to cry.

"Are you all right?"

She sniffled and nodded. "Ah-ha. These are happy tears. What can I say? I'm a crier. I'm sure you've noticed that by now. I cry and I cry and I cry. I cry when I'm sad. And I cry when I'm happy. But right now, I'm crying because this is what true romance is all about. And some people think that romance is like a unicorn—something that only lives in the imagination."

"Well, we know that unicorns exist because we both saw one," he said.

She giggled through her tears.

Finally, she pushed him back down, flat on his back. "We're going to feel what it's like to be free. We're both going to feel what real freedom is like because we're going to give it to each other. Okay?"

"Okay."

She slipped her panties down her legs and kicked them off with her right leg. Positioning herself so that most of her weight was on her right side, she straddled him and slowly impaled herself on his cock. She squinted her eyes and breathed through her mouth when he entered her. When he was completely inside her, she threw her head back and massaged her own breasts. He reached up and caressed her boobs as well. She grabbed his hands and they interlocked fingers.

She leaned forward to kiss him, and as she did, the Star of David pendant that she was wearing contacted the gold crucifix that he had on. The sound they made was like that of two champagne glasses being clinked together during a toast. So much so that she looked down at him, warmly smiled, and said, "Oh! Cheers!" They both laughed.

Then she started moving her hips, side to side, rotating, grinding. "You're really tight," he told her. She looked down at him and his compliment inspired her all the more.

"I want you as deep into me as you can get," she told him.

"You're the most beautiful woman in the world. You're special."

She stopped for a moment. The words moved her because she knew that he was sincere. The love she felt was transferred into a passion. She had never felt herself so sexually charged before.

"I'm going to thrust down on you and I want you to thrust up on me. Know what I mean?"

He nodded.

She began to ride him, and she rode him hard. The sounds of flesh meeting flesh filled the room and added to their passion. "That's it, baby! Get into me! Get *into* me!" she told him in a husky, guttural voice. Her hands clutched his chest and her nails inadvertently dug into him, cutting him. It was a very minor cut, but a cut nonetheless. Neither of them even noticed though.

Little yips escaped from her lips and she fell forward, and her bar of soap promptly smacked him in the face with a dull thud. This snapped them both out of their mutual passion trance.

"Oh, my God, are you okay?"

He glanced down and saw the small cut on his chest and told her, "I guess you like it rough, huh?" He laughed and rolled her over.

"Ouch!" He inadvertently hit her bad ankle with his leg.

"Sorry about that. You okay?"

"Um-hum, I think so. Maybe we should have a paramedic standing by whenever we make love," she told him. They both laughed.

He briefly moved to the bottom of the bed and gently lifted her left leg and looked at her ankle. "That's a pretty little ankle that you have there," he told her. He kissed it and then climbed on top of her, careful not to touch her left leg. She could feel his penis, warm and throbbing, pressing against her stomach. He kissed the nape of her neck and massaged her right breast.

Her body and mind were overwhelmed with the stimuli. Goosebumps, butterflies in her stomach, her skin was flushed. She even felt lightheaded. Instinctively, she was thrusting her hips upwards.

"Get back inside me. I need you inside me again," she begged.

He entered her and began thrusting downward to meet her upward thrust. They had a good rhythm going. She looked up at him with big eyes and he tenderly caressed her cheeks with his large hands. Then he kissed her, and their tongues wrestled one another. All she could think was that this was the most intense physical experience she had ever had. The sexual equivalent of standing atop Mount Everest. All of her senses where activated and heightened. She could smell the scent of his cologne, mixed with the scent of her perfume, mixed with what smelled like lavender scented dryer sheets that had been used on the bedding. She heard the sloppy sounds of flesh-on-flesh. She opened her eyes and focused on his blue eyes. And when their kiss ended, he sang to her. In a voice as tender as the lyrics themselves, he sang *Loving You.*

As they made love, one thought consumed her — *this is what must have happened behind closed doors in all those old movies. This was the part that they never showed you on camera, the part that was always left to the imagination.*

She felt his body tense up and he plunged deep into her and kept pressing like he was trying to fuse their bodies together. He was coming. She could feel it. After the spasms stopped, he resumed his thrusts, this time with even more force and speed. Finally, a particularly deep thrust triggered sensations that began at her cervix and rippled throughout her entire body, like waves from the epicenter of a tsunami. Her body shuddered and she threw her head back, closed her eyes, grabbed the baby blue bedsheets with her nails, and vocalized some sounds that weren't even words, just primal grunts.

Eventually, she opened one eye. She patted his chest and in a breathless voice said, "You tapped my cervix, dude."

"Oh, gee, I'm sorry."

"No, no, no. That's a good thing," she assured him.

"It is?" He finally stopped thrusting but was still inside her.

"Yeah, it is. It's the most intense kind of orgasm a woman can have."

"So . . . it was good for you? I mean . . . I did okay? That's very important to me. I want to please you."

"You did. That was the best I've felt in a long, long time. I think it may have even gotten my creative juices flowing."

"I think it got other juices flowing, too." He laughed.

"Again, with the comedy."

He kissed her on the forehead. "It was wonderful." Then he flashed an ornery grin. "Heck, this felt better than the Orioles winning the World Series." He very quickly winked at her.

She wagged her finger at him. "Don't you even joke about that, David O'Malley. Don't you compare making love to baseball. As much as I love baseball, it can't compete with romance." To emphasize her point, she took her pillow and playfully smacked him in the face with it.

He nodded agreement and ran his hand through her hair. "I know. You're right, of course. I promise to never bring up baseball again in bed."

"Thank you." She thought for a moment, got a mischievous grin on her face and raised her eyebrows. "Now, what do you say we play a doubleheader? I know you just pitched a perfect game, but I want to play again," she told him, as she looked at him with pouty lips.

He smiled and pulled the sheets over top of them and started kissing her neck again and she squealed with delight. And they made love again.

Chapter Ten: Broken Teddy Bears

David awoke to the distinct smell of pancakes and sausage. He put on a pair of shorts and a t-shirt and went down to the kitchen. There, he found all the other members of the household gathered. Rain Man and Brandi were sharing scraps of sausage Hannah had put down for them. She stood over the stove's burner flipping hotcakes. She was wearing only her black bra and panties. He looked at her as she stood there with her left foot held slightly off the floor. In his mind, she couldn't have looked sexier. He walked up behind her and put his arms around her waist and startled her.

"Oh, God! I didn't even hear you come downstairs. You scared me."

"Sorry. You should have woken me up. I would have made breakfast for you."

"You're sweet."

He kissed her neck. "And you're sexy." He massaged her breasts through her bra. She threw her head back and took a deep breath. "Not so shy anymore, huh?"

"No need to be. I feel closer to you than I've ever felt to anyone," he told her.

"I'm honored that you feel that way," she said as she flipped a hotcake.

He turned her around and looked deep into her eyes. "It scares me a little."

"And why is that?"

"Because I feel closer to you than I do God."

"God is love so what difference does it make?"

He smiled down at her, then hugged her. She was so soft and warm and comforting. And she smelled so good, a mixture of her perfume and the pancakes and sausage. He didn't want to let go of her. "You sit down," he said. "I'll finish making breakfast."

She sat at the kitchen table and checked her phone.

After a few minutes, the food was done and he prepared a plate and set it in front of her.

"Thank you," she said.

With one hand she continued to scroll on her phone and with the other she cut her stack of pancakes.

"The video we posted of Bobby and Babs on YouTube is getting some reaction," she announced.

"What are people saying?"

"Some of the comments are very supportive and some are rude and ignorant."

"That's to be expected," he said.

"I know. But it still bothers me when people say cruel things."

"Anytime you try to do some good there's bound to be a certain amount of resistance," he said.

She nodded. "I suppose." Then she looked up the clip of them dancing. "Oh, by the way, the video of us at Tiffany's is up to half a million views now," she told him. She showed him the comment from Amanda's mom.

His eyes got big. "Wow. I don't even know what to say to that. That's pretty heady stuff when someone tells you that you've helped restore their *faith in humanity*."

"I know. I was tempted to respond to let her know that we saw her comment, but I don't know what to say."

"Don't overthink it. Say what's in your heart."

She pushed her pancakes around her plate with her fork to saturate them in syrup as she thought and took a sip of her coffee. "I'll tell her that love heals and that we are honored that our love has helped her begin to heal."

"That's wonderful. Perfect, in fact. That's the perfect response."

They went out onto the beach to have a smoke. She put on a white terrycloth robe and he went out in his shorts and t-shirt, despite the cold.

"We should send the video I took of you singing *Caged Lions Never Roar* to the Finally Free Foundation, along with the video we took of Bobby and Babs. It would add even more of an emotional punch."

"Oh, I . . . I don't like the way I sound when I sing," she said.

"Nonsense. You have a lovely voice. It conveys sweetness and sincerity. You're a very talented lady."

"You're not just saying that because you're my boyfriend, are you?"

"No, of course not. If you sucked, I'd tell you."

"So you'd tell me that I *sucked*?"

"Totally." He thought that was the right answer, but it was a trick question.

"I can't believe that you'd be so callous to tell me that I sucked. I mean, you could say *needs some work, has potential*, but *sucks*? *Sucks*?"

"There wasn't really a right answer to this question, was there?" he asked.

She brushed his nose with the tip of her index finger and smiled. "Nope."

They put down their smokes and he kissed her, then he scooped her up and set her down in the sand. He climbed on top of her and gently used his index finger to trace her lips. She grabbed his finger and put it in her mouth and sucked on it.

"Sex on the beach is more than just a drink, you know,"

he laughingly told her.

She spat his finger out of her mouth and said, "David, there's someone watching us. Turn around — there's some lady standing on the back porch."

He looked over his shoulder. It was one Mrs. Karen Aumiller, the bishop's personal secretary. And spy. Mrs. Aumiller was a tall, thin woman in her 50's who was prone to sending nasty emails to the clergy on such important topics as the need to set the default on all Diocesan printers to black and white to save money. *Oh shit! What does that shrew want?*

"Who is that woman and why is she standing there staring at us?"

"It's the bishop's secretary. You stay here, and I'll go talk to her."

He walked to the porch. "Karen, how are you doing?"

Mrs. Aumiller looked him up and down and then looked down to the beach at Hannah. "Not as well as you. I see you have a guest."

"Yes, well, that's my friend, Hannah."

"Oh, I've seen the two of you together, on social media and on television, cavorting and making spectacles of yourselves. When I was growing up in the Church, you would never have seen a priest carry on like that."

He was on the verge of losing his temper. "What, ah, what brings you here, Karen?"

"Some nuns are having a retreat here later this month and I'm here to take inventory, to see what they need. I rang the bell at the front door but no one answered. I would have come at a better time if I had known you were so, shall we say, *indisposed*."

He smiled. *That's it. If she wants some juicy gossip to take back, I'll give her some.* "I guess by *indisposed* you're referring to the fact that Hannah and I were getting ready to have sex right here on the beach, huh?"

Mrs. Aumiller gasped and covered her hand with her mouth.

"We had sex last night, you know. All night long, in fact. Yep, right there in that house owned by the Diocese. Yeppers. Sex was had right in there." He pointed up to the house.

"Oh, Dear Lord! Why I've never—"

"And that's part of your problem, Karen. But I can't help you with that."

She turned around and stormed away.

As she left, he yelled out to her, "You can tell Bishop Higgins all about our conversation. I know you will anyway. And while you're at it, you can tell him that she's Jewish. He'll get a kick out of that." He shook his head as he walked back down to the beach.

"That didn't go well, did it?" she asked.

He threw his hands up in anger. "She shows up here unannounced. God knows how long she was standing there watching us! I shouldn't have said what I said to her, but I get tired of all this *holier than thou* hypocrisy."

"I'm sorry about this. I feel like it's my fault."

He put his arm around her. "Not your fault. These old fuddy-duddies don't want anyone to have a life, that's all. I guess they want everyone to be as miserable as they are."

She gently brushed his hair with her hand. "Ice cream," she told him.

"Say again?"

"*Ice cream*. When you're down, ice cream always helps to lift your spirits. There's a great ice cream place on the boardwalk. When they open, let's get some."

"Sure. And we can stop by the arcade and play some games."

"Will you win me a teddy bear? They have that one game where you throw the ball and knock down the pins. For a former professional baseball player who pitched, that game shouldn't even be a challenge."

"I sense sarcasm in your voice," he said.

"It's just that you have a torn rotator cuff and all."

"Oh, ye of little faith. You've heard about how the Catholics have *Touchdown Jesus* at Notre Dame. Well, we Anglicans have *Strikeout Jesus*."

They went inside and took a shower together. He watched as she took her soap-on-a-rope off her wrist and scrubbed her body. She saw him staring at it and preempted him. "I'll tell you all about the soap-on-a-rope. I will, David. The time just has to be right, okay?"

He sighed. "Okay." *That's got to be a hell of a story.*

They got dressed. She wore grey sweatpants and a red Washington Capitals hoodie, and white sneakers. He marveled at how sexy she could look in such a simple outfit.

He wore jeans, a white turtleneck, and a green mohair sweater and a pair of tan, suede Hush Puppies.

The boardwalk was perfect that day. Bright sun, temperatures warmed to the mid 60's. There were people out, but it wasn't too crowded.

He couldn't win her the teddy bear on the ball toss, though he spent thirty dollars trying to win what looked like a ten-dollar bear. "These games are rigged in the house's favor," he insisted. But at Skee-Ball, he won enough tickets to get her a faux diamond ring. He put it on her left ring finger. It fit perfectly.

"You like it?" he asked.

She opened her hand and stretched out her fingers to admire it. "I do," she said with great deliberation and purpose. After a short pause, she asked, "Do you think it looks good on me?"

"I do."

They stopped to get ice cream. He got pistachio and she

got peanut butter crunch.

When they walked back to the car, they passed a city trashcan that was overflowing with garbage.

"What? Is the Sanitation Department on strike or something?" he sarcastically asked.

On top of the pile was a discarded teddy bear. He was all brown and wore baby blue overhauls. One of his eyes was missing and stuffing was coming out of numerous holes in his body. He wore a smile on his face that was especially poignant, given his situation.

Hannah stopped when she saw him. "Oh, look!" She set down her crutches and picked the bear up. "Look. Someone tossed him away."

"Well, he's just an old teddy bear, an inanimate object."

"David! Haven't you ever read *The Velveteen Rabbit*?" she asked.

"It's a story. A fictitious story."

"I know. But, still, there seems to be something so wrong about someone just throwing him out like this. He's sad. I'm going to keep him. He can be fixed. Get him a new eye. Replace his stuffing. He could be as good as new."

He looked on as she brushed the bear off and tried to clean some catsup off his forehead. Some guys might think she was crazy. But he thought only a very exceptional human being would pick a dirty, damaged teddy bear out of the trash because she felt sorry for it. As she used the rest of the small pack of tissues that he had given her to try to get the catsup off, he pitched in and did his best to push the bear's stuffing back into its belly.

"I guess you got your teddy bear after all," he told her.

She looked at the bear and hugged it. "I know you think I'm silly, maybe even nuts. But just think—this bear was once loved. He was once a child's prized toy, was probably held by that child every night. Nothing that has been loved and cherished should ever be thrown away simply because it's imperfect. Things that are good don't stop being good because of a few blemishes here and there."

They stopped at The Dugout, a sports memorabilia shop at the south end of the boardwalk. She insisted on going in by herself and made him wait outside. When she came out, she was carrying a small, brown bag but she wouldn't reveal what was inside.

They rode the tram to the far end of the boardwalk to have lunch at Sharky's, a little seafood place with outstanding crab cakes.

Then it happened. First, there was a catcall. Then a voice bellowed, "Well—well—well, if it isn't Sabrina Sinn! Almost didn't recognize you with your clothes on, girl!" It was Kevin, one of the regulars from Polecats. He was wearing a t-shirt that had a red cross on it and said *Orgasm Donor* and the men's version of a pair of Daisy Dukes. Before Hannah could even turn around, he had already come up from behind her and smacked her ass and cackled about it.

"When you coming back, Sabrina? You're the best piece of meat in that place."

David stood between Hannah and Kevin. "What the hell are you doing, pal?" he asked.

"Just saying *hi* to my girl, Sabrina. Step off, dude!"

"You've got the wrong person, buddy. *You* need to step off." David reached for his cellphone. "I'm calling the police. That was a sexual assault."

She intervened. "No! No! I . . . I don't want to get the police involved. Let's just drop it, David. He mistook me for someone else, that's all. Let's just get out of here."

David threw up his hands. "*Just drop it*? What are you talking about? I'm not going to let this asshole get away with touching you that way."

"David, *please*. I don't want to press charges. Now, come

on—let's go!"

He reluctantly put away his phone.

Kevin looked at him and grinned a shit-eating grin. "Oh, I get it. You're banging that, huh? You're screwing her, right? Good for you, bro. I envy you. Every guy in Baltimore wants to hit that."

David grabbed him by the collar and threw him to the ground. Kevin looked up at him with a mixture of fear and recognition. "Wait a second! Aren't you some type of preacher, a minister or something? Yeah! You did a service once at the Maryland State Penitentiary when the prison chaplain was on vacation. I remember. Hey, you're supposed to love people not beat them up." Kevin flashed the peace sign.

David held on to Kevin's collar and cocked his left hand, getting ready to punch him in the face with a left cross. "I'm going to show you some *tough love*, my son."

Kevin's eyes flashed panic. "Jesus wouldn't hit me! He was a pacifist. WWJD?"

David stared into his eyes, his hand still cocked and ready to deliver the blow. *Even the Devil can quote Scripture when it serves his purpose.* Finally, he let go of Kevin's collar and gradually unclenched his fist. He rose to his feet and ordered Kevin to get up, too.

"Apologize to the lady. Or I'll call your probation officer."

"Shit, ain't no need to get my proby involved in this little misunderstanding."

"Then apologize!"

Kevin looked at her. She had her head down. "Okay—Okay. I'm sorry."

David prompted him further. "No. Say *I'm sorry, ma'am.* Call her *ma'am.*"

"I'm sorry *ma'am.* There. I said it. Now you won't call my proby, right?"

"Go!"

Kevin picked up his Jesus sandals that had fallen off in the scuffle and power walked away from the scene, occasionally looking over his shoulder, until he finally disappeared into a vape shop.

A small crowd had gathered to watch the altercation. David casually told them, "It's okay folks. We were just rehearsing for a play our church is putting on called *The Bible In Action*. It's kind of a Jesus meets Chuck Norris type of thing. Experimental theater. Very edgy, very avant-garde."

After the crowd dispersed, he went over to Hannah. She had tears in her eyes.

"Are you okay?"

She put her head in her hands and took deep breaths. "Let's just go."

"I wish I would have punched him. If I had to do it over, I would belt him." A moment later he added, "I guess he did mistake you for someone else, huh? Sabrina Sinn—sounds like a bad porn name." She said nothing.

She took the soap off her wrist. "I need to get to the nearest restroom. Now."

"Are you hurt?"

"I don't feel well." She was hyperventilating.

They found a nearby lady's room. He waited outside, nervously smoking. Ten minutes passed.

Finally, an older lady came out and asked, "Is that blonde in there your wife?"

"My girlfriend."

"Well, something's wrong. She's in the shower, the one they have for washing the sand off, and she's crying. You should go in. I can stand out here and make sure no one else goes in." He nodded and entered.

She had taken her clothes off and was sitting in the shower crying and scrubbing her skin as lukewarm water poured down on her.

"What's going on?"

"I'm dirty."

"What do you mean?"

"I'm dirty. That's why I carry this soap with me."

He walked into the shower and turned the water off.

"No! I'm not clean enough yet. Turn it on!" She looked up at him with a defeated look on her face. "I'm sorry," she said. She reached up and turned the water back on.

She insisted on scrubbing herself for another ten minutes. When she finally got out of the shower, he went outside and borrowed a beach towel from the lady who was standing watch and help her dry off and get dressed.

As they drove back to the house, he told her, "I have to know what's going on. I have to be able to understand what just happened. When we get back to the house, we need to have a talk, okay?"

She put her head down and nodded. "Okay. Yeah. We'll talk."

When they got back, he fed the animals and then they went out to the back porch. Each lit up a cigarette.

She held up her wrist and looked at the soap. "Some people have an albatross around their neck. I have a bar of soap around my wrist."

"But why do you have it?"

"Because I can't *not* have it. I would freak out. I mean, I guess I have a form of OCD. Certain things trigger it. Sometimes, I feel dirty. And when I feel that way, my mind tells me that the only way to feel even semi-normal is to take a shower and scrub myself clean. The soap-on-a-rope—it's almost become a part of me now. It's very hard for me to be without it. I can only be without it if I have no choice. Because I never know when I'm going to feel dirty. Have you ever felt that way? Have you ever felt dirty?"

"I remember once, during a hurricane, I lost power for a week and couldn't shower. I felt really dirty."

"Okay, but that's just being physically dirty. I'm talking about being emotionally dirty."

"You can't blame yourself for that man assaulting you. You didn't do anything to prompt that."

"Maybe not. But I've made choices in life that have created this situation."

He took the cigarette out of his mouth and took her cigarette out of her hand and set them both in an ashtray. Then he placed his hands on her shoulders.

"You're one of the best people I've ever met in life," he said.

She put her head down and shook it. "I might not be worthy of that pedestal that you have me sitting on."

"And what's that supposed to mean?"

"It means that you don't know all there is to know about me."

"So what else is there to know?"

She kept her head down. "I strip."

"You strip what? Paint? Strip mine? What do you strip?"

"My clothes. I strip off my clothes. I'm a professional stripper. An exotic dancer. A *polecat*."

He smiled. "You're putting me on, right? This is all an elaborate joke, right?"

"I'm afraid not. I'm afraid that I'm completely serious."

His smile faded, and his stomach felt queasy. He felt like he was going to be physically ill.

"You told me you're a *hostess* at a *nightclub*."

"Well ... you could kind of make the case that that's true."

"Oh, for God's sake, that's splitting hairs! That's what a politician would say! You owed it to me to tell me this from the start!" He was shouting.

She shouted back. "Well, what was I supposed to do? Wear a sign around my neck saying *I'm a stripper*?"

"I don't know if I can deal with this, if I can be with someone who takes her clothes off in front of strangers for money. Don't you understand that you're not only stripping your clothes off but you're also stripping yourself of your dignity?"

"Yes! I do understand that! I hate it! Goddammit, I hate it! And I hate myself. I hate it when those dirty, filthy slime balls stare at me and touch me. Do you think today was the first time I've been assaulted like that? I hurt my ankle falling off the stage after I kicked an asshole for grabbing my breast. The bastard tried to make a joke out of it, told me that his favorite magician is *David Cop-A-Feel*. I never wanted this life for myself—I sort of stumbled into it and never quite knew how to get out."

"I don't even know what to say to you right now."

She grabbed his hands and held them. "Listen to me! I'm going to quit. I've already made that decision. *You* helped me find the confidence in myself to believe that I could be a writer."

"It's good that you're quitting but the damage is already done. Decisions have consequences."

"Isn't that what forgiveness is for?"

He shook his head, took a deep breath and exhaled. "Look, I can forgive but I can't—"

She interjected, "Forget. You can't forget. I get it."

"You're trying to make me out to be the bad guy here, but I'm not the one who lied. I'm not the one who works in the sex trade. And what else are you doing besides stripping?"

"If you're implying that I'm turning tricks, you're dead wrong! I've never sold myself."

"You sell yourself every time you walk out onto that stage."

"I thought you were different. I thought you loved me, that you'd see me for who I'm trying to be instead of who I've been. I had the nerve to think that your love for me was stronger than any sense of self-righteousness that you clung to."

"It's not that simple. I'm a member of the clergy, for God's sake! Do you know how it will look when people find out that I'm with someone who was a stripper?"

"Why does it even matter what it looks like? Why does it even matter how our relationship appears to the rest of the world?"

"Because no relationship exists in a vacuum and perceptions become reality."

"All that matters is that I want a better life for myself. And I want you as a part of that. I *love* you. That's the only reality I know. And I've never spoken truer words in my life."

"But I believe in fidelity."

She got a quizzical look on her face and threw her hands up in exasperation. She screamed at him. "I believe in it, too! *One-hundred percent!* Why the hell are you even bringing that up? What—are you trying to say that I'm some kind of *slut* now? I've never slept around. Never!"

"But you don't understand. Every time we'd be together, I would think about all those other guys who have seen your body, who have ogled you, who have touched you, even if it was uninvited."

"I think about those things nearly twenty-four seven! That's why I scrub my skin raw with this damn bar of soap. I'm a prisoner to those thoughts! I have no control over the past and neither do you. Why dwell on it? People waste so much time being bitter over things they can't change." She lowered her voice and put her arms around his waist. "Don't be that way, David. Please don't be that way. You're better than that. I know you are." He pulled away from her.

"It's different for guys. It's . . . it's emotional. You're making a rational argument about an emotional issue."

"I'm the same person I was a few hours ago. Nothing has changed."

"Bullshit! A lot has changed. You dropped the romantic equivalent of an atomic bomb on me. How can you expect me to be all nonchalant about that?"

"I didn't expect you to be nonchalant. But I did expect us to be able to work through this."

"Uh-huh. And what about my job, hmm? I'm already on thin ice with the bishop and if it gets out that I'm dating a stripper, they'll fire me."

"So all that talk about being free enough to not care about what others think—that was all bullshit, I guess, huh?"

"For God's sake—this is reality. We're not having some philosophical discussion in a diner."

"So that's all it was to you? Words that sounded noble but were never meant to be put into action? If that's the case, those words were meaningless. *Meaningless!* Words only matter if they're backed up by action!"

"You're not living in the real world."

"Oh, I'm living in the *real world* all right. But I wish I wasn't because the real world sucks! It's full of people who lock lions up in tiny cages. And toss disabled cats out in the streets to fend for themselves. *And guys who give girls rings that they won playing Skee-Ball—rings that are supposed to symbolize something—then betray that girl's love.*"

"Listen, I'm the one who was betrayed here."

She looked into his eyes. "Look, I am sorry if I hurt you. I am sorry that I didn't tell you sooner. I am sorry I've made some bad decisions in life. I'm sorry! I'm sorry! I'm sorry! But I *do* love you. Now, you either want me or you don't. Make the choice."

"Oh, so now you're giving me an ultimatum? You spring

this shit on me out of left field and then you want to give me ultimatums? Don't you understand? I could lose everything. My career, my standing in the community, my reputation . . ."

"So you're ashamed of me?"

"I'm ashamed of what you've been doing for a living. Yes!"

"So! Am! I! I've admitted that! I've apologized. *Mea Culpa,* Your Holiness!" She paused, shook her head, then added, "You're not the man I thought you were. You're what Nicki said you'd be. Like all the rest of them. I want you to take me and Rain Man home. After all, a woman of my ill repute shouldn't be contaminating a church-owned house with her presence. Remember—you're supposed to be a man who helps people strengthen their faith. Well, you've destroyed mine. I have no idea how you walk on water with those feet of clay."

She took her faux diamond and threw it at him. "Here's your stupid ring back. I don't want it." She glared at him. "You said you'd never hurt me. And I was foolish enough to believe you."

The long ride home was filled with deafening silence. When they got to her townhouse, he tried to help her with her luggage and Rain Man's carrier, but she would have none of it. She hastily gathered her things, crying all the while. In his carrier, Rain Man cried along with her, stressed by the long car ride. After she was done, she screamed at him through the car's window. "I hate you! Love scorned, hate born! I know it's a sin to hate but I guess I'm already a sinner. Because you've judged me so." He shook his head and rolled up the window and started to pull out of the driveway.

She gingerly walked to her front door, stopped, turned

around and walked back to his car and motioned for him to roll down the front passenger's window. "Oh, and one more thing—you most definitely *are* a cad! The caddiest of cads, in fact!"

Before he rolled up the window, he yelled back. "*Caddiest.* That's not even a word, little Miss English major!"

She flipped him double birds, went inside, and slammed the door.

CHAPTER ELEVEN: SOMETHING TO RE-MEMBER YOU BY

On Friday, David stopped by the local dry cleaner and picked up his vestments and one other item. Mrs. Bunting, whose husband owned the business, worked the register and did some sewing and mending on the side.

"How'd that little project come out?" he asked.

"Not bad, all things considered," she said as she pulled a plastic shopping bag out from under the register. She pulled Hannah's teddy bear out of the bag and proudly detailed her work.

"I went ahead and replaced both eyes, since the other one was getting ready to fall off, too. I pulled out all the old stuffing and replaced it. His innards are all brand new. He had quite a few holes in him. The hardest one to fix was the one right over his little heart. I guess what they say is true — *a heart is the most difficult thing to mend*, even in teddy bears. But he's in good shape now. He even smells good. I soaked him in a mild cleaning solution after I patched him up."

David inspected the bear. It was quality work. He was pleased with the results and nodded approvingly. "How much do I owe you?"

"The dry cleaning came to forty and the bear came to fifteen."

He handed her a crisp one-hundred-dollar bill. As she checked it with a counterfeit pen, she asked, "Can I ask you why you didn't go out and buy a brand-new teddy bear? I mean, you could buy one of comparable size for about ten dollars."

"Yeah. I know. This one kind of has sentimental value. You see, he belongs to a friend of mine. She intended to get him fixed but then she inadvertently left him in my car. Anyway, I'm not sure if I'll ever be in a position to get him back to her or not, but I wanted to get him patched up. Getting him fixed was important to her, so I figured that's the least I could do." He forced an uneasy smile. "It just seemed like the right thing to do."

Later that afternoon, he went for a walk with Brandi. They walked the St. Anne's churchyard and looked at the graves of American and British soldiers who had been killed—who had killed one another—at the Battle of Baltimore during the War of 1812. They lay side by side. Enemies in life. Neighbors in death. They were sharing eternity together, whatever its composition.

They walked into the Church. St. Anne's was an old Colonial Era church. The ceiling was high, and red carpeting adorned the floor. It smelled of incense. They walked up to the altar and he looked at the life-sized crucifix that hung on the wall above it. In a few hours, the Church choir would arrive for practice. But when he and Brandi walked in, it was quiet, save for the dull hum of the heating system.

"I don't really talk to You much this way," David began. "What I mean, is that I talk to You but it's not really talking. It's more like rote, regurgitation of what other people think are proper things to say to You. But what I'm really looking for is a dialogue. I need answers. Just plain talk. No *thees* and *thous*, please. You see, I don't know what to do. I . . . I feel conflicted. Maybe that's how You felt in the Garden of Gethsemane that one night . . . not that I'm comparing myself to You, mind you. Or my situation to Yours. But I feel awful. In the pit of my stomach, I feel a queasy kind of pain. It literally hurts. You see, I *really do* love her. But there's more to life than just love. I mean—come on. There are real, practical matters that you have to think about, right? Having a job *matters*. Being respected in the community that you serve *matters*. What people think *matters*. Yes! It *does* matter. You *know* that. Please do me the courtesy of at least admitting that much. And then there's the whole matter of knowing how many other guys have seen her. Naked. As naked as Eve. I hate that thought. It makes me angry to think about other guys seeing her that way. That should be for my eyes only, you know? Well, I guess You don't know. It's kind of a guy thing, a *human* guy thing. But it bothers me that she's done what she's done. Even though she says she's going to quit, it still bothers me. Part of me thinks that whenever I'd look at her, I'd always see *Sabrina Sinn* instead of Hannah Cohen. Part of me sees her as tainted, I guess. There's a part of me that can't get all this stuff out of my mind, can't move beyond it.

"Why do You make it so hard to do the right thing? I need You to send me some Light, and I need it bad. I need a sign because I can't figure this one out on my own. And I should tell you—sometimes I doubt that You're even there. At times like this, yes, I do have doubts. Any thinking person would. There. I said it. To Your face, no less. Part of me wonders right now whether I'm just talking to myself.

"I need a sign. You know, speak to me somehow. Something to show me The Way, if there even is a Way. Or maybe I'm too far lost to even find the Way."

From above, he heard a deep but kind voice. "It's not that complicated. The word *love* is both a noun and a verb. So in other words—if you love her, then love her."

He got goosebumps and his heart raced. Slowly, feeling both awe and fear, he looked upwards, towards the organ loft, where the voice was emanating from.

Standing at the railing in front of the organ was an old man with a scruffy beard and long silver hair pulled back in a ponytail. He wore dirty blue jeans riddled with holes, a dirty t-shirt that advertised a physical therapy clinic, and a black ball cap with yellow lettering that said *Vietnam Combat Veteran*. Embedded in the cap was a pin depicting the Rampant Lion of the 28th Infantry Regiment.

David took a deep breath. "You startled me, sir. For a moment, I thought I was getting a message from above."

The old man smiled to reveal he was missing several teeth, including one of his front ones. He laughed a belly laugh that threw him into a coughing fit, then he hocked up some phlegm and wiped it from his mouth with an old red and white checkered handkerchief. Once he stabilized himself he said, "Thought the musings of an old homeless soldier were some divine words of wisdom, did you?"

David smiled. "For a split second, you had me wondering."

The man smiled and nodded. "Ah-ha."

David heard the sound of nails on the hardwood floor and the man gingerly bent down and picked up an ancient tan and white Apple Head Chihuahua with a severe underbite. The old man held the dog close to his chest. The tiny dog—smaller than an average sized adult cat—wore an extra small navy blue doggie sweater that had a baseball ball and bat on it and said *Lil' Slugger*.

"Me and Babe here—uh, that's his name, Babe." The man pointed to the little dog before continuing, "Named after one George Herman Ruth, The Sultan of Swat, and the greatest ballplayer of all-time. Born right here in Baltimore in 1895. So anyways, me and Babe—we were out walking and noticed your church was open and we saw the sign out front saying *All Welcome*. So I says to Babe, I says *well I guess we're part of the all*. So we moseyed on in. Hope you don't mind.

I'd like to go to the library, but they won't let Babe come in with me. I already told them he's my service dog, but they say I have to have *documentation* that he's an official service dog. Well, I don't have that, see? So we can't go in."

David walked up the spiral staircase to the organ loft. As he climbed the stairs, he said, "You and your dog are welcome here anytime."

"Much obliged."

When David reached the top of the stairs, his eyes focused on a brown paper bag sitting on the floor with a black bottleneck sticking out from the top.

The old man smiled. "That's my rheumatism medicine." He laughed another belly laugh.

David smiled. "Does it work?"

"Damn right." The old man broke into a delicate and very slow soft-shoe dance which he finished off with *jazz hands*.

David laughed and clapped when he finished. "I'm Father O'Malley." He extended his hand.

They shook hands and the old man introduced himself as *Mike*. Mike admired a piano that was next to the organ. "Mind if I tickle the ivories, padre?"

"*You* play?"

"Yes. I did. A long time ago. Once upon a time, I played *Somewhere in Time*."

"Well, then, by all means, have at it." David gestured for Mike to sit down on the piano bench. Mike sat Babe on the floor, next to Brandi, and the two dogs smelled each other's butts.

Mike took a long swig from his bottle and his hands stopped trembling long enough for his fingers to dance over the keyboard. He played the theme from *Somewhere in Time*. Beautifully, he played it. He played it as if he had written it. And in a way, he had. And it was hauntingly gorgeous and full of tender regret.

David got goosebumps and tears ran down his cheeks and he didn't even know why except that perhaps it had struck him on such a basic level. An ineffable mystery, he thought. A feeling that pure, raw Beauty can sometimes bring on.

When he was finished, there was silence for several awkward seconds. Mike finally asked, very softly and thoughtfully, "Do you think that maybe somewhere in time, there's someone waiting? Someone waiting even for someone like me? Someone who would like little Apple Head Chihuahuas the way I do? Once upon a time, someone said she'd wait for me. Wait for me to get back. But she didn't. She didn't wait. And now, here I am, fifty years later. And sometimes I live in the streets. But mostly I live in my memories. Of days and times gone by. *Bid time return*, as Willie boy once wrote."

And it broke David's heart and left him speechless.

Mike cleared his throat and said, "From what I heard, you have a girl problem."

"Yes, you could say that."

"Doesn't sound like much of a problem to me."

"Is that right?"

Mike nodded emphatically. "That's right. See, I'm a simple man, at least that's what everyone tells me. So I know simple when I see it. And your problem's simple." Mike focused on David's Orioles t-shirt and continued, "Now, if you want to talk about a complicated problem, we can talk about the Orioles' starting rotation. They lost again last night. Gave up six runs in the first inning. No starting pitching on that team."

David nodded agreement. "Yep, you're right—no starting pitching. Normally I watch every game. But lately, I haven't been interested." He looked Mike up and down. Mike looked awfully thin to him. "Would you like something to eat?"

"Oh, I'm fine. I had something over at Our Daily Bread earlier. Babe and I split a hot roast beef sandwich."

"That's not enough for either of you. Wait here." David went back to the rectory and warmed up some takeout pizza in the microwave and grabbed a can of dog food and some sausage flavored dog treats. He brought the food back to the Church and watched them devour it in a matter of minutes.

After they were finished, Mike patted his stomach and said, "That was one fine meal. The only thing that's missing is a post-meal cigarette. One of the great pleasures of life, if you ask me. Ah, might I impose a bit more? After all, I wouldn't be a bum if I didn't bum a smoke." He laughed and again threw himself into a coughing conniption.

David smiled. "No imposition." He pulled out two Camels and handed one to Mike. They went outside and lit up.

Between drags, Mike wheezed up a storm. He smiled and told David, "No point in quittin' now. Damage is already done. It can't be reversed. COPD, you know."

"Sorry to hear that."

"The damage I've done to myself can't be reversed. It's too late. But the damage you're doing to yourself isn't irreversible. Yet."

"And what damage is that?"

"You care too much about what people think, and I'll bet you dollars to donuts that those people whose opinions you worry about are *assholes*. That, and you live in the past. You're a prisoner to the past, in fact."

"Prisoner to the past?" David shot him an incredulous look.

"That's right. You're letting the past determine the present and the future. You're not making very good use of that freedom that me and my buddies fought and bled for. If you keep on this path, you're liable to wind up like me. One day, you'll have *only* the past. Only memories to keep you warm

146

at night. And you'll plead with Time itself. And Time is like a stubborn, arrogant baseball umpire. It never reverses itself. Even when it knows it's been unfair. You'll *bid time return,* and Time will give you the finger and say *fuck! You!"* Mike turned his eyes upward, tipped his cap, and added, "Beg your pardon. I didn't mean any disrespect using that kind of language on Your property. Just the old soldier in me talking, that's all."

The old man looked at David. And David saw his powder blue eyes, which were the only feature Mike possessed which didn't look aged.

Mike took a long drag on his smoke and said, "Listen, son, if you love her, then love her. Because it's bigger than just you. It's a skirmish in a larger battle. But each skirmish plays a part in determining who wins the War. And if there's one thing that I know, it's war. And this War goes back to the beginning of Time itself." The old man's eyes got big. "It's *Epic*. Like a Cecil B. Demille picture. *That* kind of Epic! And everything depends on its outcome. *Everything.* Heaven and Earth and everything in between."

David thought it was the ramblings of an old man who was, perhaps, in the early stages of dementia, but he nonetheless tried to decipher Mike's speech.

They finished their smoke. Mike picked Babe up and prepared to leave.

"Do you guys need a place to stay? You can stay here."

"Oh, no, no. Me and Babe — we make out. We always find someplace to stay."

"Well, do you need a ride anywhere?"

"Nope. Don't need a ride. Don't want a ride."

They shook hands and David gently shook Babe's tiny front paw. "It was a pleasure meeting both of you," he told them. David took out his wallet and handed Mike three twenty-dollar bills, which was all the cash he had on him, and told him to use it for food for himself and Babe.

Mike tucked the money in his pocket. "Much beholden to you there, padre."

David shook his head. "Nope. You're not beholden to me. As I said it's my pleasure. Really it is."

Mike dug into his pockets. "Oh, hey, I have something for you, too. Some freebies. See, when you live like me, you never turn down any freebies, even if you don't need them. It kind of becomes second nature to grab anything that someone's giving away." He pulled some items out. "Let's see here. We've got some mints, some dinner mints from the soup kitchen. An Orioles pocket schedule that I got from a convenience store. Oh, and a Gideon's Bible with a Bible verse bookmark. All yours, padre." He handed the items to David.

"Well, to be honest, Mike, I have a Bible."

"You do, do you?"

"Yeah. They kind of recommend when you take the job that you get your own. Because, you know, it's not a bad idea to be familiar with it."

"Oh, I'll be darned. I thought you worked with loaners. Well, here, take it anyhow because I don't need it. They got them all over the place down at the soup kitchen. And I don't want to throw away the Bible. That would be bad karma, and me and Babe sure don't need that."

David smiled. "Okay. Sure. I'll keep it. Maybe it can make friends with some of the other Bibles here."

As Mike walked out with Babe in his arms, David asked him, "Do you ever read the Bible?"

"Sometimes. When the Spirit moves me."

"Do you have a favorite verse, something I could remember you by?" David asked.

"Yes." He said it with great deliberation and then smiled at David for a moment.

And then he turned around and walked away without saying another word. David watched him leave. He watched until he and Babe disappeared, on the other side of a hill, into the setting sun. He lit up another cigarette as he tried to make sense of his encounter with the two of them. He pulled his cell phone from his back pocket and dialed up a piano version of *Somewhere in Time* and closed his eyes and listened as he smoked.

When the song ended, he pulled the small, green Gideon's Bible out of his front pocket. He planned to put it in one of the Church's pews. The bookmark fell out and floated to the ground like a feather. He picked it up and looked at the Bible verse printed on it. Hebrews 13:2. And he looked down at Brandi as he smacked the bookmark against his palm and told her, "It's a coincidence, of course. That's all. People want to seize on coincidences and make them into something more. But they're not. Still, that little encounter would make one heck of an episode of *The Twilight Zone*." He shook his head and laughed.

Chapter Twelve: Somewhere in Time

It was Saturday and they still hadn't talked. As far as Hannah was concerned, he had made his choice. Nicki paid a visit for the post-breakup debriefing. They put a frozen pizza in the oven for dinner.

"He's like a TV commercial pizza," Nicki told Hannah as she cut through the pepperoni pie with a pizza cutter.

"TV commercial pizza?" Hannah asked.

"Yeah. You know, they make it look so freaking good on the TV commercial. The cheese is all gooey and it's got tons of toppings. And it looks so fresh. So you buy it based on the commercial. Then you get it home and find out that it tastes like shit. The cheese is all thin and processed. And there are barely any toppings on it. The crust is like cardboard. I swear, there are people in the advertising business who make a nice little living making crappy pizza look good to the masses." Nicki put a slice on Hannah's plate and then licked her fingers before continuing, "And speaking of making a living, are you still going to quit Polecats?"

"I don't see any point to it now. I'm defeated, as defeated as those lions. I may as well embrace what the world sees me as. I'm a stripper, a polecat. That's all I'll ever be. Even the man that I dared to love could only see me like that. You were right, Nicki. You said this would happen and it did. You're a real prophet."

"Well, it wasn't a difficult thing to predict. When are you coming back?"

"My ankle's healing faster than I thought it would. I think

by Monday, I'll be fine. I'm going to call Ronnie today to let him know I'll be in on Monday night."

"Atta girl!

Hannah pushed her pizza away. "You act like you're happy about this."

"Well, business has been way down since you've been out. Down by something like twenty-five percent. That's what Ronnie was saying anyways. That should flatter you. There are, after all, some guys who want you."

"Well, I don't want *them*. I'm going to get ten more cats and become the youngest Cat Lady in history." She pointed to Rain Man, who was on his side, poking his paw under the refrigerator in an attempt to retrieve a lost toy. "He's the only guy that I'll trust from now on." She sighed. "I still can't believe that he didn't want me. Or at least didn't want me enough."

Nicki shrugged her shoulders. "All's fair in love and war."

"Oh, God! How would you know? You've never been in either. What a meaningless expression anyway. Next thing I know you're going to tell me that I'm in your *thoughts and prayers*."

Nicki pointed at her. "Good one. I hate it when people say that. The people who say that generally have you in neither their thoughts nor their prayers. I've never said that because I don't pray, and I'm far too honest to use such a trite phrase anyway."

Hannah's cell phone alerted her of a new email. It was from The Finally Free Foundation. It read,

Dear Ms. Cohen,

Thank you for making us aware of the plight of Bobby and Babs. We reviewed your documentation and were appalled by the conditions at this facility. One of our Field Operators reached out to the owners of this zoo, to attempt to discuss our organization purchas-

ing both lions with the intent of relocating them to our cage-free wildlife sanctuary in Tanzania, Africa.

Our Foundation made a good-faith effort to negotiate for Bobby and Babs' freedom. However, the owner told us in no uncertain terms that our offer was "inadequate." Sadly, we were unable to reach an agreement with the zoo.

We would, however, encourage you to continue to make the public aware of these lions, and all the other animals who are suffering at this facility.

Again, we regret that we could not be of greater assistance. Should you have any questions, feel free to contact me.

Doreen Robbins, Finally Free Foundation, Big Cat Case Manager

She wanted to cry and tried, but she was all cried out. She relayed the news to Nicki and dropped her phone and said, "I'm done! I am just *so* done! I'm done fighting windmills. I've failed at everything I've ever tried. I'm wasting energy and emotions. It was stupid to think I ever had a chance. Freedom is a pipedream."

On Saturday evening, David was sprawled out on the couch, staring at the ceiling. He heard a knock at the front door. It was Bob Sterling, the Parish Council's Chairman. Bob was a heavyset man in his 40's who was prone to wearing crewneck sweaters that were always a bit too small. He wore cheap cologne even though he could afford the expensive stuff and used old school pomade in his hair. He resembled Ken Bone.

When David opened the door, Bob had a stern look on his face.

"What's going on?" David asked as he shook Bob's hand and motioned for him to come in.

"I was going to ask you the same thing," Bob said.

"Something tells me you already have an idea."

Bob nodded. "Yeah. There's no use beating around the bush. I know you're on vacation but the bishop and the Parish Council feel that an emergency Parish Council meeting is in order. We're going to meet on Monday afternoon."

"And what do you plan to discuss?" David asked.

"Something tells me you already have an idea."

"And am I invited to this meeting?"

"Oh, yes. You must be there, in fact. You'll have to answer to these allegations. One of the Council's main jobs is to hold the clergy accountable. And these are serious allegations. Very serious."

"And what have you heard?"

"Mrs. Aumiller reported what she experienced at the Diocesan House in Ocean City. And, as if that wasn't bad enough, we received a report that this young woman whom you're carrying on with is an exotic dancer to boot."

"Who told you that?

"We received an anonymous letter. So the picture we're getting is of an ordained priest who's had premarital sex in a Church-owned dwelling with a woman who takes her clothes off for a living. Now, was I wrong in anything I've said?"

"She wants to quit. She's actually very smart and wants to become a—"

Bob cut him off. "—And we've been getting calls and emails and social media posts ever since this news broke. People are threatening to stop tithing. Parents are talking about pulling their children from Sunday School and Youth Group activities. This summer's Vacation Bible School is in jeopardy. You've undermined this Parish's reputation, which it has built over the last two-hundred-fifty years. Staying loyal to the Crown during the American Revolution couldn't destroy this Church but your loyalty to this woman just might. We're the laughing stock of the Diocese. We're going to lose money and prestige over this. We already have."

"So I'm being fired? Is that it?"

"Now look, I like you, believe it or not. I think I can save your job here but you're going to have to make a public statement to the entire congregation admitting that your relationship with this woman was a serious lapse of judgment. And that you promise to never see her again, that you're severing all ties. If you do that, I think I can call off the wolves. This time."

"And what if I'm *not* willing to do those things?"

"Then we'll remove you. No question about it. So this should be an easy decision for you. Listen, if you play your cards right, one day, you could be the bishop of this Diocese. Higgins will be retiring within the next year or two. He's been talking about opening a big game hunting lodge in Texas. You're smart, young, good looking—and *yes*, looks *do* count. Articulate, too. You have the potential to bring in a lot of money to the Church, to be a good earner. But you need to learn to use better judgment and resist the urge to follow reckless impulses. Now, we'll expect you at the parish house at three o'clock on Monday. Please. Oh, and when you come to the meeting make sure you're in your clerical shirt and collar. No baseball jerseys or caps."

Bob showed himself out. David sat in stunned silence and let out a deep sigh. He looked at Brandi, shook his head, rubbed his eyes, and deeply exhaled. He pulled the bookmark the old man had given him out of his wallet. He stared at it, studied it, considered it. Then he tossed it into the trashcan. And he retrieved it a few seconds later. In his weaker or perhaps more realistic moments, he came face-to-face with his certainty that he was uncertain about most everything. He chuckled to himself and then looked up and muttered, "The fact that I've recently been doubting Your very existence hasn't stopped me from fearing You." He put the bookmark back in his wallet and got out his phone and watched the video he'd taken on the beach of Hannah singing *Caged Lions Never Roar*. And he bade time to return.

On Monday morning, he put on a pair of shorts, running shoes and a t-shirt. He went for a jog around Roland Park. His goal was to run to Pimlico and back. He always found that running helped him think, helped clear his mind. It was cloudy, and the air was humid. Storms were forecast for the afternoon—good old-fashioned April thunderstorms. The ones in Maryland weren't as bad as the ones in the Midwest but still could be quite violent when the cold air from the North clashed with the warm air coming up from the South.

As he cut through the thickness of the humid air, he approached St. Francis of Assisi Catholic Church on Blackberry Lane. There was a large crowd gathered outside. Some of them were smoking. A few were wearing cheap, polyester suits. Many of them he recognized as members of the homeless community. One man, dressed in shabby clothing, pulled his dog, an elderly, arthritic Rottweiler, around in an old, red, child's wagon. The doors to the church were open and as he jogged by, he faintly heard a piano inside playing what sounded like a familiar tune. He stopped and walked up to the front door and looked in. At the front of the church, a Franciscan nun sat at a piano and played *Somewhere in Time*. She didn't play it as well as Mike had. It was missing the sense of melancholy resignation that he had imbued it with, but she still did it justice. He walked inside and looked towards the altar. There was a plain, no-frills casket sitting on a bier. He walked up to it and peered inside the box. Lying in dignified repose was Mike. He was laid out in his Vietnam-era Army dress greens, with staff sergeant stripes on his sleeves, and the Rampant Lion patch of the 28th Infantry Regiment on the shoulder. In his right hand, he held an Orioles ball cap. And his left arm was wrapped around a dead, tan and white Apple Head Chihuahua who lay on his side, with his head propped up on Mike's left arm. Babe wore a baby blue doggie sweater that was embroidered with the words *Daddy's Little Angel*. Between his paws, was a small, yellow rubber ducky squeak toy. With the exception of his collection of doggie sweaters and t-shirts, it had been his only worldly possession.

Father Collier, the priest at St. Francis, recognized David and walked up to the casket.

"Did you know Mike and Babe, Father O'Malley?"

David wiped away sweat that was now infused with tears. "I made their acquaintance once. What . . . what happened?"

"They were spending the night in an old condemned rowhouse. The only shelter in the city that had an open bed that night wouldn't allow dogs in, and Mike would never go anywhere without Babe. Anyway, there was carbon monoxide in the house. They just . . . they just went to sleep and never woke up." Father Collier reached into the casket and gently stroked Mike's cheek and then Babe's before adding, "It's a blessing that at least they went together because neither of them would have made it without the other anyway."

"I was just talking to them the other day, on Friday." David shook his head in disbelief.

Father Collier got a quizzical look on his face. "Friday? You have your dates confused, Father O'Malley."

"Oh, no, it was Friday, Friday afternoon. I'm quite positive. We talked. He gave me some advice and gifts."

"Then perhaps it was a different homeless man and a different dog."

"No. It was Mike and Babe. I'm absolutely certain."

"Father O'Malley, Mike and Babe died *ten days ago*. It's taken this long to bury them because they had no money, no family. We decided to step up and cover the expenses to give them a proper burial."

"Ten days ago? *Impossible*."

Father Collier pulled out the obituary and pointed to the date of death.

David's heart raced, and he started to hyperventilate. He stumbled and had to steady himself by holding on to one of the casket's handles.

"Are you all right, Father O'Malley? You don't look well. Maybe you should sit down and have some water."

David took a deep breath and waived Father Collier off. "I'm fine. I'm fine. But may . . . may I have a moment alone with Mike and Babe."

As Father Collier walked away, David again peered into the casket. The music was reaching its crescendo. "I hope you find that someone you were looking for. And I hope she likes animals. I'm sure she will." He chuckled to himself. "She'll have to, right? I found one who likes animals, you know? She loves animals, in fact." Then he looked at Babe. Tiny little Babe, with his endearing underbite. He gently scratched his tan ear and looked at a photograph sitting on the table next to the casket. It was a Christmas photo, the kind that they take at pet stores around the holidays. Babe was sitting on Santa's lap, in a little elf costume, with a smiling Mike kneeling by his side. And it touched him on such a primal level, much like Mike's piano playing had. He couldn't take it anymore. He lost it and openly wept. Loudly, he sobbed and wept. And he wasn't embarrassed. He was mourning his friends and he didn't care what anyone else thought. Because anyone who would have a problem with it was probably an asshole anyway. He whispered, "Why does anything ever have to die?" He thought for a moment and added, "Maybe it doesn't." Then he turned and walked away.

As he headed out the door, Father Collier stopped him.

"Are you sure you're okay, Father O'Malley? Did you ever figure out when and where you met them?"

David warmly smiled and nodded. "Somewhere in time. I met them somewhere in time." He turned and walked out the door without saying another word.

Chapter Thirteen: The Book of Revelation

Later on Monday afternoon, David stood on his front porch. Mr. Benjamin, who owned a small apartment building next to the Church, was mowing his lawn. For the first time that spring, David took in the scent of fresh cut grass.

Soon, he'd have to get ready for the meeting. Before he went, he decided to have a smoke. He pulled out a cigarette and searched for his lighter. Frantically, he searched for it, but it wasn't in his pockets. *Shit, there's nothing worse than jonesing for a smoke and you can't find a light.* He was pretty sure there was one somewhere in the car. As he walked to the vehicle, he noticed it was getting dark. It looked like twilight, despite the fact that it was only midafternoon. The very tops of the still barren trees began to sway.

He searched the car for a lighter. He checked the center console and the glove box. Then he looked under the seats. He found petrified French fries, an expired coupon for a free cup of coffee from his favorite convenience store, and an overdue library book, the one which he swore on his reputation as a member of the clergy that he had returned. Under the passenger's seat, he found a small orange lighter. *Thank God!*

Next to it was a pink diary. It had fallen out of Hannah's purse on the ride back from the ocean, he reasoned. He pulled it out along with the lighter. After he lit his cigarette he walked up to the rectory's front porch and examined the book. It was well worn, and the title was printed with a homemade label maker and affixed to the cover. The spine was in bad shape and some of the pages were loose. There was a small, brown paper bag sticking out from the top, like a bookmark. He took the bag out and peeked inside. It was a commemorative Roy Hobbs baseball card, signed by Robert Redford. She had bought it for him in Ocean City, he deduced. He looked at it and smiled. Dragging on the cigarette, he read the title of the book aloud to himself. *"Hannah's Handbook: Musings of a Hopeless Romantic."* He went to tuck the loose pages back inside and dropped it. Several pages broke free from the spine and floated to the ground. The wind, which had picked up even more, started blowing the pages around the porch. He had to hustle to collect them all before they blew away. As he tried to put the pages back in the proper order, his eyes caught a glimpse of the entry entitled *Hannah's Song*. He read it. Part of him felt guilty for reading someone's diary entry but he justified it by virtue of the fact that the pages, quite by accident, were out and before his eyes.

As he read, as he absorbed her words, he knew that such words could only come from that part of the heart where Loneliness and Beauty occasionally intersect. He decided that only those two forces colliding could produce something so exquisitely sad. And he knew that such words could only be harvested by a pure and gentle soul. The type that chose disabled cats over normal ones, fetched broken teddy bears out of the trash, and dreamed up stories about barren, lifeless worlds transformed by the power of love. He felt ashamed. He felt like a zookeeper, like old man Rupert himself because not all cages are made of steel and have finite boundaries.

He put the pages back in the diary, making sure that they

were all in the correct order. After he finished his cigarette, he went inside and took a shower, then headed over to the parish house. He grabbed his umbrella and made the short walk from the rectory. It was raining, and windy enough that his umbrella turned inside out. The rain blew horizontal and an occasional lightning bolt was hurled from the sky. It was only about a twenty-second walk, but he was still soaked.

When he walked into the building, he could smell freshly brewed coffee and he could feel everyone's eyes on him. He surveyed the room. They were all there, all thirteen of them, plus the bishop. David sat in the front of the room, behind a long table that they used for spaghetti dinners. The bishop sat next to him at the table, while members of the Council sat in grey folding chairs.

The bishop gave an invocation. He uttered something about asking God to bless them with the "ability to discern Your most perfect Will for both Father O'Malley and this Parish." Typical Higgins bullshit, David thought.

The bishop then summarized the allegations, telling them, "This incident is about the ability of this Church and even this Diocese to remain credible and relevant within the community. Father O'Malley has taken pleasure in flouting the Church's conventions and teachings for some time now. I have made a sincere attempt to counsel and even mentor him. But instead of improving, what we've seen is that he continues to deviate even farther from Church teaching. Now, mind you, I have no ill will towards David. I love him as the Lord commands us to love even those who are misguided. But the question before this Committee today is whether or not he's qualified to continue to lead this congregation. Remember, this is a man who by his own admission engaged in sexual relations outside of marriage and did so on Church property.

"Moreover, it's been alleged in the form of an anonymous complaint that the woman involved is an *exotic dancer*, society's euphemism for a stripper. His continued presence here will only further damage the reputation of this Parish. You'll lose members and money as a result. And the loss of those resources will confound the Parish's ability to do the Lord's work. Remember, this is not about whether Father O'Malley is *likable*. It's about competency and credibility."

The bishop pointed at David. "Would *you* be comfortable with this man teaching your children Sunday School?" The bishop was smooth and articulate, like an ace prosecutor. He looked at David and asked, "For the record, Father O'Malley, have my statements been accurate? Have I summarized the facts fairly?"

David cleared his throat and looked at each person in the room. "The basic facts, as told by Bishop Higgins, are accurate." There were some low murmurs and rumblings in the room. He could even hear a *Sweet Jesus!* uttered under someone's breath.

Higgins cut him off. "The facts speak for themselves. There's no context that makes this somehow okay." The bishop rose and started pacing back and forth in front of the Committee members. Lightning struck outside, and the lights flickered. The wind-blown rain tapped on the stained-glass windows. "Sadly, David's continued ministry here is untenable. It would be in his best interest and in the best interest of the Church for him to leave this Parish and reconsider his vocation altogether. It causes me great pain to say this. Believe me, I take no pleasure recommending his removal. But I would be negligent in my duties if I did not take this stance. Someone, after all, has to stand up for God. You see, people like Father O'Malley want the Church to take the position that *anything goes*. He believes in a watered-down form of religion, one in which the Ten Commandments become the *Ten Suggestions*. Well, by God, I'll never tolerate that as long as I'm the bishop of this Diocese. Not everything is relative. And I'll tell you something else—"

Arms crossed, David rolled his eyes and interrupted. "I never said *everything is relative*. That's a strawman argument. Now, if you'd let me explain."

Higgins raised his voice and shook his head in disgust. "*I am talking, please!* No manners! And you show no respect, either." He quickly regained his composure and looked at each member of the Council. "Don't forget 1 Corinthians 5:11, which warns about keeping company with those who are sexually immoral. You have an obligation to this congregation and to God Himself to act decisively to remove this man from his duties here."

They asked David to leave the room, so they could discuss his fate freely among themselves. In the next room, he sipped on black coffee. At one point he heard someone banging with a fist on the table. He was certain that that was the bishop making an emphatic point about what a danger he was. He did his best to tune out the voices, did his best not to hear what was being said about him.

Finally, after about a half hour, Bob Sterling called for him to come back into the room. As he walked in, heads turned in response to a large tree branch which fell outside as a result of the winds.

Bob turned to David and began, "Bishop Higgins raised some serious concerns regarding your continued ministry. Frankly, he made a good case for your removal. You admit to the allegations, and I didn't detect any remorse. Still, you've been here for a couple of years now and some here believe you've done some good work. We've come to a compromise. Our desire is to see you remain so long as you sever all ties with this woman and issue a public apology for your behavior to this congregation. It's crucial that you say that your behavior was wrong, and a lapse of judgment. A simple mistake. Now, this is a very generous offer." Bob looked at the bishop. "Some would say it's too generous. But that's our offer. Now, what do you have to say for yourself?"

David rose, put his hands in his pockets, sat on the table, and looked out at his accusers. "You know, I became a priest because I wanted to do something important. Something that mattered. But more and more it seems like everyone is playing a game, and I'm wondering how much God there really is at work here. I see people within this Church, some in this very room, who profess devout faith in God but conduct their lives as if He doesn't exist. As if it's all just a game. A product to be sold, both literally and figuratively, by a big corporation called *The Church*. And I wonder if the Carpenter, the poor, transient carpenter, would even recognize or claim this institution that's been set up in His name.

"Indulge me while I tell you some things about my friend, Hannah. Yes, that's right. She has a name. Hannah Cohen. And she's the kindest person I've ever met. I've learned more about God from being with her than I ever did in seminary or in this Church. She rescues discarded cats from animal shelters and discarded teddy bears from trashcans. She cries over lions who've been locked up in tiny cages in the name of the almighty dollar and then works to set them free. She writes beautiful songs and poetry. And one day, she's going to write a wonderful novel. She likes old movies, too. Old, sappy love stories. Oh, and one more thing—she knows that you can strikeout Bam-Bam Bradford if you throw him a good changeup or slider.

"I'm telling you these things because none of you have ever met her. Of course, that hasn't stopped you from judging her. It must be wonderful to know the Mind of God the way you all do, to have a direct line of communication. More often than not, He leaves me guessing, to be honest. Only once in a very great while does He grant me a moment of clarity. But He did recently. And the one thing that I do know as an absolute certainty is that I love Hannah Cohen. And because I love her, I'm going to love her, if she'll still let me. Because the word *love* is both a noun and a verb. If you love someone, you have to love them. Let the record show that when push came to shove, I chose love. And that's what we all should choose. And I'm comfortable with God judging me based on that choice. And that, ladies and gentlemen, is my final sermon as an ordained priest. You don't have to fire me. Because *I quit*. I don't belong here. I don't want to play church anymore."

He walked out of the room, which had fallen silent. But outside, the storm still raged and was getting more violent. He walked onto the parish house porch. Bishop Higgins followed. There was a crackle, followed by a bolt of blue lightning that struck nearby.

The bishop smiled a sly smile. "Threw it all away, didn't you? Of course, I can understand your attraction to her. She's quite striking. I know. I've seen her. As much of her as you have. She's spunky, too, delivers quite a kick with those little feet of hers. Hell, I'd fuck her but that's about all I'd do with her. She is, after all, a *Jew*."

David looked at him with astonishment and rage.

The bishop continued, "My shoulder still hurts. But don't worry—I won't sue. I'm sure it will heal by the time I go on my African safari later this year and won't interfere with my ability to fire my hunting rifle. You see, I'll be hunting lions. As you may already know, I don't particularly care for cats—big or small. Yes indeed! A lion head hanging above the mantle of my den would be the crown jewel of all hunting trophies." The bishop laughed a diabolical laugh before continuing. "And if you're wondering who wrote the anonymous letter to the Parish Council . . . *Mea culpa*. It gives me

great pleasure to be able to tell you that. And if you're thinking of telling the Council, go right ahead. They'll never believe you. You have no credibility left around here. Now,
you're just a disgruntled former employee. You'll forever be
the priest who chose a stripper over the Church. *My* reputation, on the other hand, is impeccable. Oh, and, ah, when
you see her again, please tell her that my favorite magician is
still *David Cop-A-Feel.* Now go run to your little *Jewess
whore."* The bishop again laughed.

David grabbed him and threw him down onto the porch's
wooden floor. The horizontal rain was getting both of them
wet. He grabbed the bishop by his Roman collar and cocked
his left hand

The bishop looked up, smiled and chastised him. "Now!
Now! Remember what the Lord said about violence. Mat-
thew 26:53 *all who take up the sword shall perish by the sword.*
WWJD?"

David looked at him and hesitated. He slowly unclenched
his fist. For several tense seconds, neither man said anything. They stared at one another, both sweating and breathing heavy. David could see the arrogance on the bishop's
face. Finally, he again clinched his fist and delivered a powerful left cross to the bishop's jaw. And it felt good.

"Romans 3:23, Bishop Higgins. *We all fall short of the Glory
of God.* Of course, some fall shorter than others." With that,
David climbed off him and calmly walked out the door as
the bishop spat a bloody molar out of his mouth.

He texted Hannah and asked that she meet him at the
Zoo, so he could return her diary to her. The zoo would be
the best place to meet, he explained, since it was *neutral terri-
tory* and roughly halfway between the two houses.

She texted back — *mail it to me! I don't want to see you!*

He responded by explaining that a recent turn of events
was sure to impact his financial status and it would be more

sensible for him to return the item to her in person, thus saving on the postage. It would be the last request he'd ever make of her, he promised.

She agreed, telling him that she had to go to work at Polecats and didn't have much time.

Outside, it was getting darker still. Low, black clouds drifted by. One off in the distance looked as if it was trying to rotate. A few moments later, an eerie orange hue of sunlight attempted to break through the clouds, giving it a surreal feel. It was still raining hard.

When she arrived at the zoo, he wasn't in the parking lot. He was supposed to meet her there. That was the rendezvous point. But his car was there. She was wearing blue jeans, sneakers, her Orioles cap, and a royal blue hoodie that depicted Kevin the Minion eating a banana. She had her black umbrella. From her wrist, hung her bar of soap. In her vehicle was a duffle bag with her *work clothes* packed inside.

She paid the fifteen dollar admission fee and muttered to herself, "I can't believe I'm paying to get my own diary back. This guy's a piece of work."

He was over at the lion exhibit and he was talking to old man Rupert himself. She had never seen Rupert in person, only his photo. He had a pale, craggily face and wore a white suit, bolo tie, and a white cowboy hat. He had an umbrella, but he was still soaked. So was David.

As she waited for the two men to finish their conversation, she rolled her eyes, crossed her arms, and impatiently tapped her toe. Finally, he finished with Rupert and walked over to her.

Smiling, he pointed to her sweatshirt and said, "Kevin says *Bello!*"

"You have such a stupid, juvenile sense of humor," she

lectured.

He looked her up and down. "How have you been?"

"Fine. Just fine. Not that you would care."

"It's good to see you," he said.

"Uh-huh. I'm sure."

"How's the ankle?"

"Fine. I'm going back to work tonight."

"You're going back to Polecats?"

"Yes."

"Thought you hated it."

"I do. But I'm tired of fighting. Every battle I fight I lose anyway. So I decided to be what the world expects me to be."

He nodded. "I see."

"I guess you heard about Bobby and Babs. The Finally Free Foundation tried, but they couldn't get old man Rupert to sell," she said.

"Yeah. They sent me the same email. That old man Rupert is a tough nut to crack, he drives a hard bargain." He pulled out a plastic bag. "Oh, here's your diary. I also found a Roy Hobbs baseball card. You must have bought it down in Ocean City."

"Yeah, well, that was supposed to be a gift for you."

"Yeah, I figured as much, but I didn't want to be presumptuous."

"Oh, how polite of you. You don't mind being cruel but being presumptuous is a problem for you, eh?"

He pulled the teddy bear out. "Oh, and I got him fixed for you."

She examined the bear. "He looks good. Good as new, in fact."

He nodded agreement. "Yep. Just like you said he could be."

She put the bear back in the bag and clutched it against

her chest.

The rain was now coming down so hard they nearly had to shout when they spoke.

"Listen, I have to go. I'm going to be late for work." She turned around and started to walk away.

"Hold on. I need to tell you something."

With her back still turned to him, she screamed, *"What? What do you need to say?"*

"I made a deal with Rupert for the lions."

She slowly turned around. "What?"

"I bought Bobby and Babs with the understanding that their custody will be turned over to the Finally Free Foundation. They'll relocate them to their cage-free wildlife sanctuary in Africa. You'll get an email soon confirming it from the FFF Big Cat Case Manager."

"What kind of deal did you make? The Finally Free people already tried to buy the lions and were turned down."

He broke into his best Marlon Brando. "Yeah, but I made Rupert an offer he couldn't refuse."

"What kind of offer?"

"Fifty-thousand for the two of them. My lawyer's drawing up the contract as we speak."

"Fifty-thousand? Fifty-thousand? Wasn't that the amount of your baseball signing bonus? You . . . you gave away your signing bonus? Thought you were saving it for a rainy day."

He looked around as the storm raged. "Well, this *is* a rainy day."

"So they'll be going to Africa, living in Africa?"

"That's right. It'll take a few months to get them there. All kinds of paperwork and red tape. But they'll go to a cage-free, protected area. No crowds gawking at them, no poachers. Just peace and the chance to live the way lions are supposed to live. And Rupert can't use the money to go out and buy a new pair of lions because of that new law that went into effect prohibiting *roadside zoos* from acquiring big cats. That's why the asking price was so high. He knows he'll never be able to replace Bobby and Babs."

She put her head down. Despite the fact that her face was already wet from the wind-blown rain, he could tell that she was crying.

"That was very decent of you," she told him. "More than decent actually," she added.

The storm was reaching the zenith of its chaos. A medium sized tree branch fell and landed not more than ten feet from where they were standing.

"Look, I do have to go, David. This weather's awful, dangerous actually. Thank you for what you've done for Bobby and—"

"Hey, hold on. I have to make an important phone call." He pulled out his cellphone.

She let out a deep sigh and shook her head and under her breath muttered, "Try to thank him and he cuts you off to make a damn phone call."

Her phone was in her back pocket and it rang.

"Your butt's ringing," he told her.

"I don't have time to play these games. I need to get ready for—"

"Just answer your phone. Please. If you do that for me, you never have to do anything else for me. Ever."

She rolled her eyes but nonetheless pulled her phone out and spoke into it. "What? What do you want?"

He walked up close to her. Inches apart, they both held their phones to their ears.

Still talking into his phone, he said, "I just called to say I love you."

She stared at him, silent for the longest time. Her lower lip quivered, and she was shaking. A single tear formed and rolled down her cheek. It dripped off her face and into a mud puddle that had formed at their feet, like a lonely river flowing into the sea. Finally, she spoke. "Do you . . . do you mean it from the bottom of your heart?"

"Yeah. I do. I was wrong. I *was* a cad. I was worse than a cad, in fact. I was an asshole. But I love you, so I want to love you."

"But what about my past? What about what people will think? What changed your mind?"

"I got some good advice from a friend, one who gave me a grammar lesson. That, and I guess you could say that I read the Book of Revelation. There's a bit more to it. I'll tell you all about it someday. It would make a good book."

"Hold on. I'm going to put you on hold, okay? Hold please."

She placed him on hold and dialed her work number. "Hi. It's Hannah. Tell Ronnie I won't be in tonight. Or any other night. *I quit.*"

She hung up and took him off hold. "Okay, I'm back. And I love you, too. I have since the first time I saw —"

He took her phone away and placed both his phone and hers in the plastic bag. Then he collapsed his umbrella and took hers away and collapsed it, too, and threw them both to the ground.

The hard rain immediately soaked them. He leaned forward, and his forehead again ran into the bill of her ball cap. He threw up his hands in mock frustration and shook his head. "You tomboys—always with the ball caps. I'm not even going to do the Tomboy Turnaround this time." He took her cap off and flung it like a Frisbee. It landed in mud and was soiled. He chuckled and softly said, "I'll buy you a new one, okay? The Orioles came out with a really cool alternate cap that would look great on you. I'll get you one of those, okay?"

She kept her eyes locked on him, licked her lips, and

slowly nodded. Softly, she said, "Kay."

He ran his fingers through her wet hair and he kissed her. In the pouring rain, he kissed her. She lifted her left leg, like the actresses always did in those old movies that she so loved.

As they kissed, with her right hand, she pulled the soap off her wrist and held it by the rope. And she purposefully dropped it into the puddle that had formed at their feet. A few seconds later, a white Roman collar was dropped into the same puddle and landed on top of the soap. And as the rain finally subsided and the winds died down, the sun broke through and bathed them in a gentle cloak of orange. A rainbow formed but they didn't even take time to admire it. They just kept kissing.

EPILOGUE: FINALLY FREE

The Finally Free Wildlife Sanctuary, Tanzania, Africa, ten months later

Hannah hung up the phone after checking in with their pet sitter. She turned to David. "Kids are fine," she told him.

He nodded and looked at her in her khaki safari shorts and blouse. "You look sexy in those shorts," he said.

"Yeah?"

"Oh, yeah, girl. You're so hot you could melt the snows of Kilimanjaro."

"Oh, good Gawd! Hemingway's turning over in his grave. What an awful line. Good thing you didn't try to use that on me when we first met, or you'd had never even gotten to first base. In fact, you would have been benched, mister former pro baseball player."

He pulled her close and kissed her on the forehead. "You're beautiful. Inside and out, and I'm very proud of you. I love you, Hannah Cohen. How's that?"

"Much better," she said, as she closed her eyes and nuzzled her head against his chest.

They were living together in Hannah's Federal Hill townhouse. He had gotten a job as a local scout for the Orioles and doing color commentary on the radio broadcasts of the Bel Air Bay Cats. He was attending the Maryland School For Broadcasting, hoping to parlay that into a gig doing color commentary for big league games.

Hannah had received a contract for her novella, *The Designated Survivors: A Love Story,* from a small publisher that was willing to take a chance on a new author. No advance, only royalties but she was thrilled that her first writing project was actually going to be published.

So the trip to Africa was a celebration and an opportunity to see the fruits of their efforts. As they rode in the Land Rover over bumpy, rugged terrain, their Tanzanian guide, Kenny, told them what to expect.

"They're doing well. When they arrived, we sedated them and treated the medical issues. I'm sure they will look much healthier than you remember them. We're not going to get real close so make sure you have your field glasses ready. Oh, and your cameras. Make sure you have them ready, too. There's going to be a surprise as well," he told them with a smile.

As they drove deeper into the bush, they saw a herd of zebra and an elephant. Hannah took it all in. "This is the most beautiful place on Earth," she said.

"Some people believe that this was the site of the Garden of Eden," David told her.

"I can't think of a better place for it," she said as she looked around. "It's so pristine, uncorrupted by humans. I feel like we're intruding just by virtue of our presence. I feel like humans don't have the right to be here," she added.

"Like this place is for God Himself and the animals," David offered.

"Yes. Just like that. When God gets fed up with it all, he comes here and sits under an Acacia Tree and watches the animals and recharges His batteries. And after an afternoon of that, He's, like *okay, time to get back to work.* And I'm sure everything seems more manageable to Him."

They parked the Rover about one-hundred yards from a cluster of Acacia Trees.

"Those trees—they like to take naps in the afternoon under those trees. We have to wait to see if they'll grace us with their presence today. So relax. They could show up in five minutes or five hours. Here, they call the shots. It's all up to them," Kenny told them.

David rubbed his hands together and said, "Well, since we have some time to kill what do you say we go over some fun facts about Africa. You know, trivia."

She shot him a befuddled look. "Trivia?"

"Yeah. I'll start. Did you know, Hannah, that Africa produces more diamonds than any other continent?" David asked.

"Um, no. I . . . didn't know that," she said. *Is this what I think it is?*

"Well, it does. I happen to have an example of a beautiful African diamond right here." He pulled out a black, velvet ring box from his pocket and opened it.

She opened her mouth in awe and covered it with both hands. It was a 1 1/2 carat diamond.

"You have such lovely hands. Would you model this for me, so the ring's full beauty can be revealed?" He slipped it on her finger.

He admired the ring on her finger. "Oh, yes. That makes it stand out even more."

He helped her out of the vehicle and got down on one knee.

"Hannah, would you mind modeling that ring for me for the next, say, fifty or sixty years? Marry me, Hannah. Please. Please marry me."

She cried and nodded her head emphatically.

"Is that a *yes*? You're nodding your head but you're crying."

She laughed through her tears. "A woman is supposed to cry at this moment. If you don't cry when the man you love proposes to you, they take away your *woman card*."

"Oh, okay, so it's kind of like a female version of a guy watching *Brian's Song*. Because, with that movie, it's okay for a guy to cr — "

She interrupted. "Honey, it's a beautiful moment that can stand on its own without being reinforced by a reference to sports," she said as she wiped away tears and sniffled.

He nodded. "Right. Right. But, ah, just to confirm . . . that is a *yes*, right?"

"Yes, it's a *yes*."

Kenny quietly called them back into the Rover. "I don't mean to interrupt the moment, but this is what you came to Africa for. Here they come. Get your field glasses and cameras ready."

Bobby was the first to emerge from the tall elephant grass. He was now well over four-hundred pounds and sported a full mane. His mange had cleared up and he looked healthy and majestic. He walked up to the Acacia Tree and plopped himself down. The force of his body hitting the ground kicked up a small cloud of dust. He rolled around before licking one of his paw pads. Babs wasn't far behind. Her leg had healed, and she was now well over two-hundred and fifty pounds. She lay down beside Bobby and yawned a big yawn to reveal the largest set of teeth David and Hannah had ever seen.

Kenny whispered to them, "Now, here's your bonus. I call him *The Pride of the Pride.*

The thick, heavy elephant grass moved. Finally, a two-month-old lion cub punched his way through. He took off running toward Bobby and Babs but tripped over his own feet and went tumbling. Immediately, he got up, shook his head, and, undeterred, trotted on his way, joining his parents under the tree.

The three of them sat there in the shade, as David and Hannah snapped photos and took video and generally marveled at the lions' majesty and beauty.

"With a camera — that's the only way anyone should ever shoot lions." She noted as she took her photos.

All afternoon, they watched the cub play, while Bobby and Babs napped under the trees. They ate egg salad sandwiches on rye. Hannah had cut the bread into heart-shaped pieces.

As the sun started to set, it looked like a giant yellow dome on the horizon and the sky took on a certain shade of amber, a gentle but powerful shade of amber. It gave them chills and reminded them that there is a surreal, dreamlike nature to the African frontier.

The cub was playing with his own tail. He sneezed and frightened himself, causing him to leap to his feet and go on alert. Looking in the direction of the SUV, he extended his neck and made his best attempt at a roar. They could barely hear it. It sounded like the combination of a puppy whining and a domestic cat meowing. They all laughed.

She said, "Oh, gosh! That's the cutest thing I've ever heard."

The sounds of their cub vocalizing woke Bobby and Babs. They rose to their feet, stretched out, and shook the dirt off their coats. They had had their nap and it was time for the family to disappear back into the Wilderness. But before they left, they both stared at the Rover, stared at David and Hannah. There seemed to be a look of recognition on their faces. They looked at the two of them for the longest time without blinking. Everything got quiet. Like Nature itself knew that something Epic, something Sacred, was about to happen and wanted to show proper respect. And as the setting sun overwhelmed the landscape with its amber hue shadow, both lions extended their necks and bellowed mighty *Roars* that echoed throughout the bush. As if they were paying homage to two kindred spirits.

YOU MAY ALSO ENJOY THE FOLLOWING FROM EXTASY BOOKS INC:

Her Innocent Marine
Arthur Archambeau

Excerpt

They were bound for Seacrets, a popular club on Forty-ninth Street. As far as Ritchie was concerned, it was Danny's best chance of getting some easy and casual poontang. Well, it was his best chance short of visiting The Block in Baltimore. The Barrington cut across the Ocean City Expressway to the sounds of boyband music from the custom CD. As they turned into the nightclub parking lot, Danny could hear the club music pulsing. He was already starting to have some doubts. He wasn't into nightclubs.

"You sure this is a decent place, Ritchie?"

With an indignant tone, Ritchie countered, "Dude, the women here are fuckin' beautiful and classy as shit. I did my research. C'mon bro, have some faith in old Ritchie's judgement."

"Said the man who joined the Marines because he got expelled from college for organizing panty raids." Danny couldn't resist the opportunity to turn the tables.

"Panty raid—I'm not comfortable with that term. Makes it

sound all creepy and such. The politically correct phrase is lingerie procurement expedition." This gave Ritchie a fit of the giggles. He loved laughing at his own jokes, almost as much as he loved cavorting with skanks. Almost.

The two Marines got out of the big, gaudy Barrington and noticed there was some commotion near the club entrance. As they got closer they could see that a hooligan had a stray kitten cornered and was picking him up by the ears and tail. The black kitten was no more than two months old and was shaking with fear and wailing in distress. There was a large crowd gathered but no one was confronting the thug. Nobody wanted to get involved.

Danny immediately initiated the Marine Corps battle philosophy—aggressively press the offensive. Richie stood by at the ready for backup.

"Leave the kitten alone, asshole," Danny commanded.

"Says who?"

"Says the US Marines."

"Shove off, John Wayne. You don't wanna fuck with me. I got my education at the University of Maryland, the University of Maryland State Penitentiary, that is."

Danny, without missing a beat, launched into his best mock impersonation of The Duke. "Well, Pilgrim, I got my education at the University of Parris Island and from where I'm standing that makes me tougher than you, tough guy."

The goon swung on Danny. He ducked and delivered a powerful left hand to the gut, just as he had been taught in boot camp. The punk doubled over and was left gasping for breath, the wind knocked out of him.

Danny grabbed the kitten, stood over the downed street tough and said, "That was just a little love tap, motherfucker! Next time you do something like that I will rip off your head and piss down your neck! Get up off the deck. And for Christ's sake pull up your fuckin' pants because you look ridiculous wearin' them down past your ass. If you start lookin' like a man, maybe one day you'll act like one. Now go home and do what you do best—jack off to online porn in your apartment in mommy and daddy's basement. If you gonna come at 'Bama and the Marines, you best bring your A game, son. Roll Tide and Semper Fi."

After regaining his wind, the hood quickly disappeared into the night, leaving Danny with the kitten. The crowd began to cheer and applaud wildly. "Give 'em hell, Marine!"

As he stood there holding the tiny, precious life, he heard a voice from behind him say, "That was gallant. Truly gallant. I walked up on it just as you got there. I was going to kick him in the balls. I hate people who fuck with animals."

Danny turned and saw her. She was gorgeous in a girl next door kind of way. In fact, she was a dead ringer for a young Nancy McKeon. She was petite, about five-feet-four-inches tall, one-hundred-twenty pounds, he guessed. Her black hair was pulled back in a pony tail and her smoky doe eyes were fiery but soulful. Though it was a bit difficult to tell because she was wearing a baggy Baltimore Ravens sweatshirt, it looked like she had a big pair of breasts. In terms of female anatomy, that was his go-to. He was a dedicated boob man and made no apologies for it. The fact that he had never so much as even touched one only added to their mystique. A pair of faded blue jeans showed off a nice bubble butt, too. Outstanding.

"Thanks. I agree. Anyone who abuses an animal is a piece of shit. But now I have a real problem. I've got this kitten and I can't keep him, but he sure can't go back out on the street."

"Well, it just so happens that I'm a vet tech. I would be happy to take him. We can keep him at our clinic and get him vaccinated and neutered. When he's ready, we can find a wonderful adopter for him. By the way, I'm Beth. Beth Kelly."

"Danny Shaunessey. I'd like to do something to thank you for helping like this."

"Well, actually, I'd like to get this little guy home but I'm kind of here with a girlfriend who drove, and she won't be ready to leave for a while. Any chance you could take me home? I'm only about five minutes from here. Normally I wouldn't get into a car with someone I just met but I figure a Marine who just kicked someone's ass for abusing a helpless kitten is pretty trustworthy."

"Yeah, sure. I could do that. I just gotta tell my buddy. Can you please hold the kitten while I go inside?"

Beth gently took the kitten in her arms and held it against her bosom. As Danny walked into the club he couldn't help but wish that it was his face that was buried in her breasts.

Ritchie was already seated at a booth with three hussies and a bottle of Thunderbird that he'd smuggled in. He was regaling them with a tale of how he single-handedly wasted a dozen Al-Qaeda fighters in one firefight.

Danny pulled him away from his adoring fans long enough to advise him that he was going to take Beth home.

Ritchie gushed, "Out-fucking-standing! She's hot! I sized her up. Looks like fuckin' Jo Polniaczek. I wouldn't kick her out of bed for eatin' crackers. Now listen up—you're on the goddamned one-yard line here. You just need to cross the goal line. Do not fuck this up, boy. This is a hit-n-run raid. No emotions, no feelings. None of that bullshit. And don't worry about old Ritchie. It looks like I ain't gonna be needin' a ride back to the hotel tonight anyways . . . if you get my drift."

Danny could only shake his head as he walked away. He loved Ritchie like a brother—would lay down his life for him—but he was beginning to question his decision to get him involved in this endeavor. Desperate people do desperate things. Ritchie was good with women in the sense that he was a good talker and a lot worldlier than Danny. He had a lot of experience, but maybe it was the wrong kind of experience. The fact was, at least as it pertained to matters of the heart, Danny was about as far removed from the Ritchie Worldview as one could get.

The kitten was sound asleep in Beth's arms as they walked to Danny's vehicle.

"My car is right over here. The black Barrington."

ABOUT THE AUTHOR

Arthur Archambeau loves animals and sports. He is an avid fan of the Baltimore Orioles, Baltimore Ravens, Washington Capitals, and the University of Maryland football and basketball programs.

He attended the University of Baltimore and St. Mary's Seminary. His favorite writer is Truman Capote.